THE H

IBN-E SAFI

THE HOUSE OF FEAR

IBN-E SAFI

Translated by

Bilal Tanweer

RANDOM HOUSE INDIA

Published by Random House India in 2009

13579108642

Random House Publishers India Private Limited

MindMill Corporate Tower, 2nd Floor, Plot No 24A

Sector 16A, Noida 201301, UP

Random House Group Limited

20 Vauxhall Bridge Road

London SW1V 2SA

United Kingdom

978 81 8400 097 9

Typeset in Sabon by InoSoft Systems, Noida

Printed and bound in India by Replika Press

Contents

Introduction

LITTLE DID NUZAIRA BIBI and her husband Safiullah
know that the son born to them in 1928 would grow
up to be a master story teller. His exact date of birth
cannot be confirmed, but is believed to have been 26
July. The child's immediate milieu was humble—the
little village of Nara in the Allahabad district. His
delighted parents named him Asrar, which meant
'secrets' or 'mysteries' in Arabic.

The village of Nara where Asrar Narvi grew up had
already earned something of a reputation for learning
and culture, thanks to Nooh Narvi, an acclaimed
poet and a disciple of Daagh Dehelvi. Nara's scholarly
environment may have shaped the lives and careers
of several others: for instance, Moulvi Rehman Ali
Khan and Moulvi Ehsaan Ali Khan were renowned
hakeems whose works were used as textbooks in all
major schools of Yunani medicine. They happened to
be Asrar's maternal grand uncles. Many other poets
and scholars lived in Nara during his childhood, and
most people in the village were related. Much of this
probably influenced the young Asrar, who later said:

My father was fond of reading, therefore the
house was full of novels and ancient mythology

books but I was not allowed to even touch any of those. So I used to steal a book or two and pretending as if I was going out to play, I used to sneak up to the roof. Once on the roof, I used to be gone for the whole day. Eventually, one day I was caught red handed and the parents had an argument over it but finally the verdict was in my favor. My mother said, 'He is at least better off than the kids who spend their days playing *gilli-danda* or marbles in the streets.' Then there were no holds barred and I was completely drowned in the stories.

Asrar Narvi's secondary education brought him to the big city of Allahabad, where he found himself exposed to a far greater range of imaginative literature—from the *Tilism-e Hoshruba* to Rider Haggard's *She*. The parallel worlds of eastern and western literatures spurred his own imagination, and stories filled his mind. He was in the seventh grade when his first short story was published in the acclaimed literary magazine *Shahid*, edited by Adil Rasheed. Taken in by his mature prose style, Adil Rasheed gave the story a byline: 'A product of the thoughtfulness of the Painter of Sentiments, Hazrat Asrar Narvi.' For days afterward, the elders of the household teased him good-naturedly with orders like, 'Abay O Painter of Sentiments, fetch me a glass of water.' By the time he was in the tenth grade, Asrar had taken to poetry, and loved to be introduced as a progressive writer; and in college, he found he was already fairly well known as a poet. Later, however, he was disillusioned by the divisions, rifts and rivalries among writers.

1947 was a tough and ultimately quite unproductive year for Asrar. His confusion and mental disturbance was characteristic of his generation:

> The chain of dreams had broken. It seemed as if some wizard like Afrasiyab had caused a rain of magic knives upon all of society [a reference to the sorcerer Afrasiyab in the *Tilism-e Hoshruba*]; as if some 'she' had been charred in fire ... [a reference to Rider Haggard's *She*]; as if the coffin of ancient Kallikrates had been stoned [ancient sources identify Iktinos and Kallikrates as co-architects of the Parthenon] ... and Love would never ever reign in the Hateland again.

In 1948, he started writing satires for the monthly *Nakhat Allahabad* under the pseudonym Tughral Farghan. But he also felt he ought to try his hand at another genre. Someone challenged him that Urdu novels could not be sold without an element of sex in them. He replied that no one had ever tried. His listener then remarked that it was not possible unless an alternative genre was developed.

> Alternative? I thought for a while, and then had a vision of an eight-year-old child who had devoured all seven volumes of *Tilism-e Hoshruba*. I had also witnessed that eighty-year-

olds were as fascinated by the *Tilism* as small children. So I said to myself, all right, let me see what I can do about an alternative genre.

This was in the early fifties when literature was low on fiction, and the novel lacked novelty. Asrar's emphasis on originality and 'newness' led him to begin writing mystery novels. He assumed the pseudonym Ibn-e Safi—literally the 'son of Safi, (his father's name was Safi). Thus began the series *Jasoosi Duniya* in 1952, from Nakhat Publications. Later he moved to Pakistan, and in 1953 he began writing another set of novels called the *Imran Series*.

Gradually, Ibn-e Safi took over and Asrar Narvi faded away, still writing poetry but much less frequently than before. Ibn-e Safi wrote about two hundred and forty-five novels in both series and caused the birth of what came to be called *Anna Libraries* in India and Pakistan. These libraries helped instill a love of books in people in general. In no time at all, Ibn-e Safi's characters—Ali Imran, Colonel Faridi, Captain Hameed, Sung Hee, Thressia Bumble Bee of Bohemia, Tisdle, Dr. Dread, Finch and many others —became immortal. His novels were utterly addictive, and considered 'polite' enough for the entire family to read.

The *Imran Series* revolves around Ali Imran, an engaging protagonist indeed. He has an MSc and PhD in criminology from Oxford, but can be disarmingly moronic, even appearing mad at times. There will often be instances in the book where the reader might find his comments nonsensical. This works in Imran's favour—one would never guess that he is the Chief of the Secret Service, with the code name X2. His comic behaviour and mannerisms make him the butt of his team members' jokes and banter, and they routinely ridicule him, never suspecting that the boss they are terrified of is actually Imran himself. Imran is a past master at foiling conspiracies and unearthing sinister plots. But he is not simply an efficient detective with the uncanny ability to dodge bullets; he is as educated as he is agile, and fluent in several languages.

Jasoosi Duniya, on the other hand, revolves around Colonel Ahmad Kamal Faridi and his sidekick Captain Sajid Hameed. Faridi is well-built, tall and attractive, and his physical strength is central to most of his adventures. Faridi works for the police department merely for the thrill of it—he is otherwise heir to a huge estate, and does not need to work for a living. Despite many chances to move up in his career, Faridi declines all promotions and stays in the active service in order to avoid being assigned an administrative job. Faridi drives the latest imported cars, and even maintains a well-equipped laboratory at home to satisfy his scientific curiosity. His kennel and snake house have the finest of dogs and rarest of snakes. His assistant, Captain Hameed, is playful, mischievous, carefree, romantic, and when occasion demands, hardworking, brave, fearless, intelligent and smart. Hameed calls Faridi, 'Father Hardstone' because he never openly displays his emotions, and appears to be immune to the advances of the fairer sex.

Astonishingly, Ibn-e Safi's two series still have a very wide readership. At the time they were written, learned professors, professionals, students, labourers and housewives alike would queue up at bookstalls to buy his latest books. It may have been his clever combination of wit, suspense and humour; or perhaps, the simple prose in which he explored the most complex of subjects. His novels investigated thought-provoking social and psychological issues in a manner that would make them accessible to the general public. It is hardly surprising then that editors have compiled books of quotations from Ibn-e Safi's works, which are thought to present a faithful portrait of his times. The tenor of the books invites readers to respect the law, and be peace-loving and patriotic. Nonetheless, the details of crimes and the solutions of puzzles were convincing enough for official intelligence agencies to consult him on the latest methods in the art of detection.

Ibn-e Safi was regularly chastised by the literary elite for being a 'popular' writer, and was never granted the recognition he deserved. He responded to such criticism as follows:

Whatsoever the quality of fictional literature, it is eventually a means to mental escape. Its purpose is to provide recreation of one or the other level. Just as a football player cannot be entertained by a game of chess, similarly elitist or high literature is absolutely meaningless for a big segment of our society. Then why should I

xiv

write for a few drawing rooms? Why shouldn't I write in a style which is more popular...maybe this way some high concepts may reach the common people too?

Fictional characters often reflect the persona of their creator, and Ibn-e Safi himself possessed many of the traits and qualities of Colonel Faridi and Imran. His witticisms—like Imran's—were admired by friends and intellectual rivals, and his principles were as unshakeable as Colonel Faridi's. He was a prolific writer and in his most productive years, he wrote about three or four novels a month. The stress and labour took its toll on him, and in early 1961 he suffered an attack of schizophrenia.

The next three years found him growing increasingly isolated from those around him, and during this period he could hardly write anything at all. However, he made a miraculous recovery in 1963, and returned with another novel in the *Imran Series*—*Daerh Matwalay*. The novel's first edition was launched by the ex-Interior Minister (later Prime Minister of India) Lal Bahadur Shastri, and went on to break all sales records. The demand for the book was so high that within a week a second edition was published in India. This edition was launched by the then Provincial Law Minister Ali Zaheer. In Pakistan people formed long queues to get their hands on the first copies. Bookstores in all major cities carried banners and posters announcing the great Ibn-e Safi's comeback.

Despite his forbidding, no-nonsense exterior, Ibn-e Safi was an affectionate and trusting man. Friends and family always found him pleasant and enjoyed his company. If he had a negative trait at all, it was perhaps his reluctance to hurt even his most bitter enemies and to go out of his way to help them if he thought they needed help. During his three-year absence from the literary scene, a number of impostor Safis appeared on the market with their versions of *Jasoosi Duniya* and the *Imran Series*. Even after he recovered, he did not take any legal action against any of them, saying that he was honoured that they had managed to earn a part of their livelihood by imitating his work. Once a publisher illegally published and began to sell his novels. People persuaded him to sue the publisher, and he did. Later, however, he found out that the publisher's family was in financial trouble because of the lawsuit. He immediately forgave the person concerned, and closed the case. It is believed that he even provided monetary help to the family.

For us, his children, he was more a friend than a father. With him, we could discuss any matter without hesitation. As far as disciplining us was concerned, a single look from him was enough to make us quake. He was completely against corporal punishment as a means to discipline children. Admittedly, with seven children at home, concentrating on creative work must have been difficult. Whenever our mother tried to silence us while he was working, he stopped her, saying that sometimes this too was a source of inspiration for him. He usually wrote at night, and must have slept very little as we never saw him rising late. While writing, he would lie down on his left side and use loose leaves of foolscap paper stacked on a clipboard. He preferred ball-point pens as he had to make a carbon copy of the manuscript, which would then be sent to India for simultaneous publication.

In late 1979, doctors diagnosed our father with pancreatic cancer. He became very frail but never complained. His usual reply to those who expressed their shock or grief at his failing health was: 'I was not grateful when I was in good health so now what right do I have to complain about my bad health!' He kept writing till the last day of his life. When he passed away on 26 July 1980, the manuscript of his last novel *Aakhri Aadmi* (*The Last Man*) lay by his bedside.

No writer has bettered him since in the field of Urdu crime fiction and most certainly no writer has broken his sales records in the past twenty-nine years. Ibn-e Safi's books are still being published in India and Pakistan, and today he has a strong online presence too. A Google search churns up millions of webpages with his name. English translations of his works are being attempted for the first time, and it is hoped that these will help introduce Ibn-e Safi to the world at large.

Ahmad Safi
Karachi, November 2009

THE HOUSE OF FEAR

Chapter 1

IMRAN WAS STANDING IN front of the mirror trying to knot his tie.

'Oho...' he said in a frustrated voice. 'The same problem again! Too small or too large. They are making ties all wrong these days! Damn this.' As he fidgeted, the silk tie knot slid up and tightened around his neck. His face turned red as he choked, his eyes popping out.

'Akkhh...Akhh...Khhhh,' he shouted, using the full force of his lungs, 'I am going to die! Help! Oye, Suleiman!'

A servant ran into the room. At first he did not understand what was going on because all he saw was Imran beating his thighs with his fists.

'What's happened, sahib?' he asked, perplexed.

'Oh, you son of sahib! I am dying here!'

'Aray! But...but...'

'Don't aray but-if-then with me!' Imran said, grinding his teeth. 'Loosen this!'

'But loosen what?'

'Abay, the knot on your father's shroud, you rascal! Come here! Now!'

'Why don't you tell me properly?' the servant said, annoyed.

'How am I telling you improperly, mister? You mean to say that I, meaning Ali Imran, MSc, PhD, am telling you improperly? You donkey, this is called a metaphor in English and *isti'ara* in Urdu, understand? Argue with me if you still think I am wrong. I must witness this as well now, right before my death...'

The servant looked carefully and noticed the tie and the swollen veins around the neck. This was not new for him. He had to deal with such clumsiness regularly. He disentangled the tie.

'Now,' Imran said loudly as soon as he was released. 'If I was saying it improperly, how did you understand what I meant?'

'My mistake, sahib!'

'Whose mistake?'

'Mine.'

'Prove to me that it was your mistake.' Imran fell on the sofa, staring at his servant.

Suleiman scratched his head.

'Do you have lice in your hair?' Imran asked him angrily.

'No, sir.'

'Then why are you scratching your head?'

'No reason.'

'Stupid. Imbecile. You waste your energy doing useless things!'

Suleiman remained quiet.

'Have you read Jung's works on psychology?'

Suleiman shook his head.

'Do you even know the spelling of Jung?'

'No, sahib,' Suleiman said in an irritated voice.

'Good. Learn it now. J-U-N-G. Many illiterates read him as Jang, and some as Joong. Those who suffer from a literary diarrhea use the French 'J'. But Jung was not French. It's "Yoong".'

'Will you eat chicken or *batair*[1] for dinner?' the servant asked.

'Half *titar*, half *batair*!'[2] Imran said, irritated. 'Yes, so what was I saying?'

'You were saying that we should cook the spices till they turn red,' the servant said in a deadpan tone.

'Yes! And always cook on a low flame,' said Imran. 'And don't turn the ladle so wildly in the pot that its clanking will arouse the neighbours' desires for our food. By the way, can you tell me: where was I dressing up to go?'

'Sir,' the servant said cautiously, 'I think you were going out to buy me cloth for my shalwar kameez. Pure Bis Hazaar cotton and Boski for my kameez.'[3]

'Good. You are a very loyal and smart servant. I'd forget everything if you didn't remind me.'

'Should I tie the knot of your tie, sir?' Suleiman asked in a deferential tone.

---

[1] *Batair*: partridge.

[2] *Titar*: quail. The Urdu expression '*Aadha titar aadha batair*' means being committed to two opposite things, or being ambivalent about something. It also means half-breed, not as a racial slur but in a pejorative sense anyway.

[3] Bis Hazaar refers to a type of cotton available at that time. Boski is a variety of silk.

'Tie it.'

As he was tying the knot, Suleiman muttered in his ears again. 'Pure Bis Hazaar cotton. I can write a note for you if you want?'

'That would be very good,' Imran said.

After tying the tie, the servant wrote something in pencil on a piece of paper and offered it to him.

'Not like this.' Imran pointed to his chest. 'Pin it here.'

The servant pinned the note on Imran's chest.

'Now I will remember,' said Imran as he left the room. He crossed the room into the drawing room where three girls were seated.

'Excellent, Imran bhai is here!' exclaimed one of them, Jamila. 'You made us wait so long. Did you take so much time just to put on your clothes?'

'Oh, so you were waiting for me?'

'Why, didn't you promise us an hour ago that we'd go to the movies?'

'Movies? What movies? I was actually going out to get for Suleiman...' Imran said, pointing to the note on his chest.

'Pure Bis Hazaar cotton and Boski,' Jamila read out the note. 'What does this mean?'

The girls began to laugh. Imran's sister Surayya also came closer to see the note, but the third one kept sitting. She was Surayya's new friend.

'What is this?' Surayya asked Imran, pointing to the note.

'I am going out to buy some cloth for Suleiman's shalwar kameez.'

6

'But then why did you promise us?' Surayya asked, annoyed.

'What a nuisance!' Imran jerked his neck. 'Now who is honest here: you or Suleiman? How am I to know?'

'That servant! Consider him honest! Who am I anyway?' Surayya turned to her friends. 'Let's go out by ourselves. And besides, if we go with him something embarrassing is sure to occur. He will certainly end up committing some folly or the other.'

'My dear girls, look here now,' Imran said in a pleading voice, making a doleful face. 'This is my younger sister. She considers me an imbecile. Surayya, I will die soon, very soon, while knotting some tie. And don't blame poor Suleiman for anything. He saved my life. I am indebted to him.'

Jamila was alarmed. 'What happened?'

'I didn't tie my tie correctly and I could have died,' Imran said in a serious tone.

Jamila started laughing, but Surayya was not amused. Her new friend was also utterly perplexed.

'If you want, I can come to the movies with you,' Imran finally conceded. 'But remember, on our way back, you must remind me of the note pinned to my chest.'

'I don't wish to go any more,' Surayya declared.

'But no! It will not be much fun without Imran bhai,' Jamila protested.

'Long live, my dear!' Imran said to her triumphantly. 'Right now, I would trade Surayya for you. I wish you were my sister. I don't like this moody girl at all.'

7

'You are moody! And I don't like you either!' Surayya said.

'Look at her now. This is my younger sister.'

Jamila finally broke in. 'Tell you what,' she said. 'Keep this note in your pocket. I will remind you on our way back.'

Imran put the piece of paper in his pocket. Surayya looked a little sulky. As soon as they reached the porch, a bike came through the gate and stopped in front of them. A heavy-set, handsome man was riding it.

'Hello, Super Fayyaz!' Imran shouted enthusiastically, raising both his hands.

'Imran, my boy. Are you going somewhere?' he asked and immediately turned to the girls. 'Oh, please excuse us, ladies, but this is very important. Imran, get on the bike, hurry up.'

Imran immediately leapt onto the backseat and the bike sputtered out of the gate.

'Did you see that?' Surayya said, biting her lower lip.

'Who was that?' Jamila asked.

'The Intelligence Bureau's Superintendent, Fayyaz,' she said. 'I cannot understand why he is interested in a nutcase like Imran bhai. He often takes him along with him.'

'Imran bhai is a very interesting person,' Jamila said. 'At least, I enjoy his company very much.'

'Crazy people think alike,' Surayya said, making a face.

'He doesn't appear crazy to me,' Surayya's new friend remarked.

And her assessment was correct. Imran's appearance belied his actions. In fact, he looked quite an attractive and well-built young man. His age was around twenty eight. After completing his MSc from a local university, he went to England where he did a PhD in sciences. Imran's father, Rahman, was the Director General of the Intelligence Bureau. Upon Imran's return from England, Rahman wanted to get his son a good post, but Imran was not interested. Sometimes he would talk of starting a business in scientific equipment, sometimes of starting a science institute, but he would not make up his mind. Everyone in the family was unhappy with his attitude. He had started acting like an absentminded fool, especially after his return from England, so much so that even the servants took advantage of him all the time. They even went to the extent of stealing ten rupee notes from his pockets without Imran ever discovering them.

His father could not bear to see his face. He had grown tired of him despite the fact that Imran was his only son. It was only because of his mother that he was allowed to stay in the house. Otherwise, he would have been kicked out a long time ago.

'The only time he doesn't appear crazy is when he is silent,' Surayya said. 'You'll find out if you are with him for a couple of hours.'

'Does he bite as well?' Jamila smiled.

'Keep up your interest in him. You will find out for yourself,' Surayya said, curling her lips.

Chapter 2

CAPTAIN FAYYAZ'S BIKE WAS moving quite fast. Imran was in the backseat muttering to himself, 'Pure cotton for shalwar...Shalwar for boskon and cotty for shameez...What, what am I saying? Fayyaz...Fayyaz, please stop.'

Fayyaz pulled up the bike on the side.

'I have forgotten,' said Imran.

'What have you forgotten?'

'I made a mistake.'

'What mistake?' Fayyaz said in an irritated voice. 'Don't try to fool me, Imran.'

Imran paid no heed to his words and got off the bike. 'I think I made a mistake.'

'We are in a hurry, Imran,' Fayyaz said impatiently, turning towards him.

Imran returned to the bike, but he sat in the opposite direction: with his back leaning against Fayyaz's back.

Fayyaz said, annoyed, 'You want me to look like an idiot? Sit straight.'

'Straight? Am I sitting on my head now?'

'Please, my friend,' Fayyaz pleaded. 'People will laugh at us.'

'That's a good thing, isn't it?'

'You will fall on your face on the road.'

'If that's what fate has ordained for me, then I, an ordinary man, am powerless,' Imran replied, speaking like a dervish.

'May God help you.' Fayyaz ground his teeth and started the bike. It was a spectacle: both of them sitting on the bike facing opposite directions. Imran bent down towards his end as though he was driving a bike as well. Pedestrians laughed at them as they went by.

'Aha!' Imran chuckled, 'See I remember now! Pure cotton for shalwar and Boski for kameez. I was telling you earlier that I had made some mistake.'

'Imran, why do you consider me a fool? You shouldn't act like a madman in front of me at least.'

'Madman? You are the madman!' Imran retorted.

'What do you gain by masquerading as a fool?'

'Masquerade!' Imran exclaimed. 'This word reminds of something I should have thought of a year ago...'

Fayyaz did not reply. The bike was running at full throttle.

'Hain?' Imran said suddenly. 'Why is this bike going the other way? Oh, and where is the handle?' He started shouting, 'Help! Save me! I cannot look backwards.'

Fayyaz stopped the bike and glanced embarrassedly at the pedestrians.

'Thank God, the bike has stopped by itself,' Imran said as he got off. 'Oh God! Now I see. The handle

11

is on the rear end! They're making bikes with fronts at the back these days...'

'Why are you being such a pain, Imran?' Fayyaz said, giving up.

'You are being a pain making me ride a bike made the wrong way. What would happen if there was an accident?'

'Get on the bike,' Fayyaz pulled him back on and kick-started the bike.

'Now it seems all right,' Imran muttered.

The bike was now out of the city and had entered a deserted area, but Imran did not bother asking where they were heading.

'I need your help,' Fayyaz said to him.

'But I am very poor these days,' Imran replied.

'Do you think I am asking you for money?'

'I don't know. I thought so. Aray baap! I forgot again. Cotton pyjamas and Boski shirt! Imran, you are a fool!'

'Imran!' Fayyaz turned to him.

'Oh, yes?'

'Why do you think everyone else is an idiot?'

'Because, er...please drive on the smooth side of the road, my friend.'

'You should put an end to all this nonsense and get down to some serious work.'

'Serious, hmm. I think I remember something about seriousness...'

'Go to hell!'

'All right.' Imran nodded his head obediently.

Their bike stopped in front of a large building.

12

Three or four police constables could be seen guarding its gates.

'Get off,' Fayyaz said.

'And I was thinking you were going to make me ride the handle now,' Imran said.

They were in a rural area not too far from the city. The building in front of them was the only large house in that area, which mainly had mud houses. It was constructed in the old style. Its high walls were made of redbrick. They stood facing a large gate, which, it seemed, was the main entrance to the building.

Captain Fayyaz grabbed Imran's hand and they entered the building. Imran still did not ask where he was being taken. They walked through a long hall and reached a room. Suddenly Imran covered his eyes and turned his face away. He had just seen a dead body lying on the ground with blood all around it.

'*Inna lillahi wa' inna illai'hi raaji'un*,'[1] Imran said in a trembling voice. 'May God bless his relatives and give him patience to deal with the tragedy of his own death...'

'I have not brought you here to recite prayers,' Fayyaz said.

'You could have asked me for burial donations at my house. You did not have to drag me here.'

---

[1] This Arabic phrase literally means: 'Truly we belong to Allah and truly to Him shall we return.' Its usage varies but is recited most often by Muslims on hearing of a calamity, for example, someone's death.

'Yaar, Imran, please. Don't annoy me. I consider you a good friend,' Fayyaz said.

'Likewise. But I will not be able to give you more than five rupees. I still have to buy botton cure for shalwar… boskon…no…what was that? See, I forgot again.'

Fayyaz ignored him. After a pause he said, 'This building has been closed for the past five years. Don't you find it a little strange that there is a dead body here?'

Imran shook his head, 'No. Not at all. I would have found it strange if you had found it under a pear tree.'

'Please be serious.'

'I am already delirious.'

'I said serious, not delirious.'

Imran was looking intently at the body. He murmured, 'Three wounds.'

Fayyaz was happy to see him settle into the right mood. 'Now here is the full story…'

'Wait,' Imran bent over the body. After inspecting the wounds carefully, he looked up. 'Before telling me the full story, tell me what you know about this body.'

'It was found at twelve o' clock,' Fayyaz reported.

'Anything else?' Imran looked at him inquisitively.

'And what else?'

'But, Sheikh Chilli the Second, meaning Ali Imran, MSc, PhD thinks a little differently about this.'[2]

'And what is that?'

'You will consider me a fool multiplied by two.'

---

[2] Sheikh Chilli is a common fool in Indian folktales.

'Aray baba, tell me.'

'Listen: the murderer struck once. Then measured a distance of five inches from the wound and struck again. And then he measured the same distance again and struck the third time. He was also careful about striking in one straight line—not an inch up or down.'

'What nonsense!' Fayyaz replied.

'Measure it, my dear. If I am wrong, wring my neck. Or, put my neck on a ring.'

Imran picked up a straw lying on the ground and placed it in between the wounds. Fayyaz looked at him in amazement.

'Here.' Imran handed the stick to him. 'If this straw doesn't turn out to be five inches, then find one in someone's beard.'[3]

'But what does it all mean?' Fayyaz asked thoughtfully.

'It means the murderer and the murdered were lovers.'

'Imran, my dear friend, please be serious.'

'This stick tells you this story, which is exactly what old Urdu poets also thought. Pick up any collection, you will find at least a few poems confirming what I have just said. Here listen to this one:

Be careful while strangling me—you may sprain your wrist

for I too, am a little tough, my love...'

---

[3] A play on the Urdu phrase '*Chor ki daarhi mein tinka*'.

15

'What rubbish! If you don't want to help me, just say so,' Fayyaz said angrily.

'You have measured the distance, right? Now tell me, what can explain this?' Imran said.

Fayyaz did not have an answer.

'Think,' said Imran. 'In Urdu poetry, only a lover can allow his beloved to kill him in whatever manner she pleases. Mince his meat or strike skilfully, measuring the distance between each wound. These wounds are not a result of haste. The body does not show any signs of a struggle either. It seems as though the body quietly suffered the blows of the beloved.'

Fayyaz was quiet for a while. Then he said, 'This building has been empty for five years. But it is opened for a few hours on Thursdays.'

'Why?'

'Actually, there is a grave here. It is known that it is the grave of a martyr. So every Thursday a guy comes here to sweep and clean the grave.'

'There must be offerings on this grave as well?' Imran inquired.

'No. No such thing. The people who own this building live in the city. I have close relations with them. They have asked this man to look after this grave. There is no rush of followers on this gravesite either. When the cleaner came here this afternoon, he saw this body.'

'The door was locked?' Imran asked.

'Yes. He said he did not lose the keys and there are no signs that someone came in by scaling the wall or anything like that.'

'Then this body must have dropped from the sky,' Imran asserted. 'In fact, it would be better if you ask for help from this martyr whose grave...'

'Are you losing your mind again?' Fayyaz said.

'Who are the owners of this building and what kind of people are they?' Imran asked.

'That Judge sahib who is my neighbour,' Fayyaz replied.

'Ah, that same Judge sahib,' Imran slapped his chest.

'Yes, the same. Oh please, yaar. Be serious. For God's sake.'

'I cannot help you,' Imran said in a disappointed tone, 'because you did not help me.'

'I? *I* didn't help *you*?' said Fayyaz incredulously. 'I don't understand at all.'

'Why would you understand or help me? You are selfish.'

'I didn't help? I don't understand.'

'I have been asking you for the longest time to get me married to that judge's daughter!'

'Stop this garbage, please.'

'I am serious.'

'If you are serious, then you must have lost your eyesight.'

'Why?'

'That girl is blind in one eye.'

'That is precisely why I wish to marry her! Ah, she will look at me and my dogs with the same eye.'

'For the love of God, Imran. Please be serious.'

'First you will have to promise me,' Imran said.

'All right, baba, all right. I will talk to him.'

'Thank you so much. Really, that girl has done something to me. What's that phrase in Urdu, oh I forgot.'

'All right now, forget about it. Let's talk business.'

'No. Please let me think of her. Otherwise I will have hysterics.'

'Now this is real love.' Fayyaz made a face.

'*Jiyo*!'[4] Imran said, thumping his back. 'May your female partner live long! Now tell me, have you identified the body or not?'

'No. He is not a resident of this area and Judge sahib's family doesn't know him either.'

'Meaning no one recognizes him?'

'No.'

'Did you find anything which could shed some light on his identity?'

'Nothing. But wait,' Fayyaz said, moving towards a corner of the room. He came back with a leather bag in his hand. 'We found this near his body.'

Imran took the bag from him and inspected the items in it. 'Hmm. A carpenter's tools. But I wonder if these belonged to him. He doesn't appear to be a well-to-do person, but he doesn't seem to be a carpenter either.'

'Why?'

'The skin of his hands is soft. Look at his palms. There is no roughness on his palms. These hands

---

4 *Jiyo* literally means to live. In this context it is meant as a kind of a blessing resulting from an outburst of happiness.

18

can only belong to a painter or a retoucher,' Imran said.

'You still haven't told me anything useful,' Fayyaz said.

'What do you expect from a fool?' Imran laughed.

'His wounds are troubling me,' Fayyaz said.

'If you put a balm on my wounds, I will take care of these wounds for you.'

'What do you mean?'

'Judge sahib's daughter.' And then, as if he had just remembered something: 'Judge sahib must have at least one key to this house?'

'Yes, he has a key with him.'

'Has or had?'

'I didn't ask him.'

'So ask him. Now have this body removed. Ask them to pay special attention to the depths of the wounds during the postmortem.' He added, 'And if the depths of the wounds turn out to be equal, then this was done by none other than this mister martyr, who's buried here.'

'What nonsense!'

'Ask for help from Ali Imran, MSc, PhD, only when you intend to do what he tells you to do.'

'Your instructions will be followed. Anything else?'

'Yes. I want to inspect this building,' Imran said.

They returned to the same room after inspecting the whole building.

'Yes, also ask the judge why he tried to change the look of just this room, when he has left the rest of the building in the old style. See, none of the

19

walls in this building are plastered except the ones in this room.'

'I will ask him.'

'Remember to ask about the keys and oh, if you meet my one-eyed beloved recite that Ghalib line: "let someone ask my heart about your half-drawn arrow." I think Ghalib's beloved was also blind in one eye; a half-drawn arrow could only be from a single eye...'

'You are not going to tell me anything else?' Fayyaz asked.

'Yaar, you are a real favour-orbiter...orbiter...I forget the word...What was that?'

'Forgetter?'

'*Jiyo*! Yes you are a real favour forgetter. I have been spewing nonsense for so long and you tell me I haven't told you anything?'

Chapter 3

NEXT DAY CAPTAIN FAYYAZ invited Imran to his house. Numerous incidents had proved that Imran was not anything like how he appeared in public—neither a madman nor a fool—but still, just to tease him, Fayyaz invited Judge sahib's daughter as well. Fayyaz's wife also knew Imran quite well, and when Fayyaz related Imran's epic of love to her, she nearly died laughing.

Fayyaz was waiting for Imran in his drawing room. His wife and Judge sahib's one-eyed daughter, Rabia, were also present.

'Imran sahib still hasn't arrived,' she said, glancing at her wristwatch.

'What's the time?' asked Fayyaz.

'Seven-thirty.'

'He will be in this room in just two minutes,' Fayyaz smiled.

'Oh really! How?'

'Everything about him is odd. He sets particular times for his arrival. He promised to reach here at seven-thirty two. So I think right now he'll be standing somewhere around our house and looking at his watch.'

'He sounds like an odd person,' Rabia said.

'Oddest person. Call him the oddest person. He returned with a doctorate in science from England. And his behaviour, well, you will see it now. He is the oddest person of the century.'

There was a knock at the door.

Fayyaz went forward and the next moment, Imran was entering the room. Seeing the ladies, he bowed gently and then shook hands with Fayyaz.

'First of all, I think I should say, the weather was very good today,' Imran said, sitting down.

Fayyaz's wife started to laugh and Rabia quickly put on her dark glasses.

Fayyaz turned to Imran, 'Please meet Miss Rabia. She is our neighbour Judge sahib's daughter. And Rabia, this is Mr Ali Imran, the son, sahibzade of the Director of my department, General Rahman sahib.'

'Very pleased to meet you,' Imran said, smiling and then turned to Fayyaz. 'You always insert needless words in conversations…"Here in the sahibzade of Rahman sahib…" The two sahibs are clashing and it sounds awful. Instead, you could have simply said Rahmanzade…'

'I am not a literary person.' Fayyaz smiled.

The two ladies were also smiling. Then Rabia leaned towards Fayyaz's wife and said something in her ear. The two women stood up and left the room.

'Too bad,' said Imran.

'I think they have gone to the kitchen,' said Fayyaz. 'The cook is short of help today.'

'Very good,' Imran said, making a face. 'So you invited her as well?'

'Yes! And why not? I thought this was a good excuse to set up your meeting with her.'

'But I feel vexed,' Imran replied.

'Why?'

'Why is she wearing those dark glasses?'

'Obviously to hide the defect in her face.'

'Listen, mister! I will find many two-eyed beauties but I am attracted to the one-eyed one. Ah, what a thing she is! You must get her glasses off somehow, otherwise I am leaving without having dinner.'

'Stop this nonsense!'

'I am off,' Imran said, standing up.

'You are a strange man. Sit!' Fayyaz said, pushing him down.

'Get those glasses off. I will not tolerate this. Being in front of the beloved and not even getting a decent look at her.'

'Please keep your voice down,' Fayyaz said.

'I will tell her myself now.'

'What will you say?' Fayyaz nervously asked.

'The same thing I am telling you.'

'Yaar, for God's sake...'

'What's wrong with that?'

'All this was a big mistake,' mumbled Fayyaz.

'Great! So you make blunders and I pay for them? No, Fayyaz sahib. I will tell her: please take off these glasses. I am in stove with you...stove...stove? I think I have used the wrong word. Come on, what's the word?'

'Love,' Fayyaz said, making a face.

'*Jiyo*! In love with you. What will she say in reply to this?'

'She will slap you,' Fayyaz said irritably.

'Don't worry. I know the art of blocking a slap with a slap quite well. The method is exactly the same as blocking a sword with a sword.'

'Yaar, please. Don't try something stupid.'

'Speaking sensibly is an open insult to a fool. Now please call her. The state of my heart is such that I can and cannot explain it. What is it that happens with the separation of lovers, what is that word?'

'I don't know,' Fayyaz said, annoyed.

'Anyway, it must be something. I will look it up in the dictionary. By the way, my heart is pounding, hands are trembling, but those dark glasses are the obstacle between us. I cannot stand them.'

There was silence for a few moments. Imran stared at the vase on the table as though someone had just admonished him.

'I have made some new discoveries,' Fayyaz said.

'I am sure,' Imran said, nodding his head like a dunce.

'But first, I must tell you about those wounds. You were right. The depth of the wounds is exactly the same.'

'Are you dreaming?' said Imran.

'Why?' asked Fayyaz.

'Which wounds are you talking about?' Imran asked.

'Look, Imran, I am not a fool.'

'I don't know. I'd need witnesses to believe that.'

'Have you forgotten the corpse?' Fayyaz said.

'Corpse...oh...yes, yes, I remember. Those three wounds...they turned out to be of equal depth...ha!'

24

'What do you say now?' Fayyaz asked.

Imran began to drum his fingers on the table as if playing a tabla, humming the tune:

Stone and iron are not indifferent
Be careful: don't hit your head on every wall.[1]

'Can't you be serious?' Fayyaz said, exasperated.

'I will be serious if you promise to get her glasses off.'

'All right, baba. I will try. I made a mistake by inviting her.'

'Secondly, how long is it till dinner?'

'Probably half an hour. One of the servants has fallen ill.'

'Anyway, so what did you discuss with Judge sahib today?'

'This is what I was going to tell you. He has the key and secondly, he did not get this building as a family inheritance.'

'Then?' Imran was listening attentively.

'Actually, it was the property of one of his friends. And the friend had bought it from someone else. They were old friends but their jobs had distanced them. About five years ago, Judge sahib received a letter that was written to him from that very building. His friend wrote to him saying he was extremely unwell and would probably not live much longer; and he wanted to tell Judge sahib something important before dying. Judge sahib had not heard from him for almost

---

[1] *Sang-o ahan be niyaz-e gham nahin/dekh kar har diwar-o dar se sar na mila*

fifteen years, so it was extremely important for him to get there. But by the time he reached, his friend had passed away. He discovered that his friend had lived in the building, but he never found out what he wanted to say to him.' Fayyaz thought for a bit, then said, 'Yes, and I asked him about that plastered room. He didn't seem to know. However, he did say that it was the room in which his friend died.'

'Murder?' Imran inquired.

'No. Natural death. According to the people of the village, he had been ill for a long time.'

'Who did he buy this building from?'

'Why are you after this building?'

'Ask this from the respected father of my one-eyed beloved.'

'Please. Speak a bit low. What if she hears...'

'Let her hear. And besides, I am about to declare the state of my heart to her...'

'Yaar, Imran, for God's sake. What kind of a man are you?'

'Quit this nonsense,' Imran said. 'Please go and get that key from Judge sahib.'

'Oh, you mean right now?'

'This very moment.'

Fayyaz got up and left. As soon as he had gone, both the ladies entered the room.

'Where did he go?' Fayyaz's wife asked.

'To get some alcohol,' Imran said in a serious tone.

'What?' she said in shock. But then she immediately started laughing.

26

'He usually drinks a little before eating,' Imran said.

'I think you are mistaken. That is tonic water.'

'It isn't difficult to store alcohol in a bottle of tonic, is it?'

'You want to make us fight, do you?' Fayyaz's wife laughed.

'Are your eyes hurting?' Imran turned towards Rabia.

'Oh...n..n..no...' Rabia looked nervous.

'Oh, it's nothing,' Fayyaz's wife intervened. 'It's out of habit. She's not used to such bright light. That's why these glasses...'

'Oh. All right...' Imran muttered. 'What was I thinking now?'

'Probably you were thinking that Fayyaz's wife is utterly negligent, so much so that she hasn't prepared the dinner yet.'

'No, that wasn't it. One of my most serious problems is that I forget very fast. Sometimes even while thinking I forget what I was thinking. It is quite possible that I will forget who you are and where I am. My family members have to remind me constantly.'

'I know,' Fayyaz's wife said, smiling.

'I mean if I commit some folly, please don't hesitate to stop me.'

Fayyaz returned in the middle of the conversation, asking his wife, 'How long it is till dinner?'

He did not mention the key to anyone. Imran acted as though he had forgotten where he had sent Fayyaz. Dinner was served a little while later.

While eating, they noticed Imran was constantly in tears but no one ventured forth with any questions. Even Fayyaz, who claimed to know Imran intimately, couldn't understand this behaviour. Fayyaz's wife and Rabia stole looks in Imran's direction every once in a while. His tears did not cease. Imran, however, did not seem to notice his tears himself. Finally, Fayyaz's wife could not resist the temptation and she asked, 'Is something a bit too spicy for your taste?'

'No, no. Not at all.'

'Then why these tears?'

'Tears? Where?' Imran said, wiping his face with his palm. Pointing to his plate, he said, 'But this could just be the same thing, and I didn't even realize...'

'What thing?' said Fayyaz.

'The roast chicken reminds me of a distant relation of mine. His name rhymes with the word roast. That made me think about his death. Then I thought what if he is thrown into hell fire...Hell...Roast chicken...God forbid.'

'You're weird, Imran.' Fayyaz was irritated.

Judge sahib's daughter was laughing uncontrollably.

'So when did he die, this relative of yours?' asked Fayyaz's wife.

'Not yet!' said Imran and continued eating.

'Yaar, I'm afraid you'll really go mad.'

'No. As long as Coca Cola is in the market, I can't go mad.'

'Why?' asked Fayyaz's wife.

'I don't know, but this is what I feel.'

Judge sahib's daughter wanted to sit with them

after finishing the meal, but Fayyaz's wife made an excuse to take her out of the room. Perhaps Fayyaz gestured to her. As soon as she had gone, Fayyaz handed over the key to Imran. After examining it for some time, he said, 'This key has been duplicated recently. Look, it has some wax particles stuck in it. Wax mould—you know what that is, right?'

Chapter 4

THE NIGHT WAS DARK. In the sky, thick, dark clouds were drifting in circles. Cutting through the darkness, Captain Fayyaz's bike was cruising down the road. Imran was riding pillion, rolling his eyes like an owl. His lips were tightly clenched and his nostrils quivered in the breeze. Suddenly, he tapped Fayyaz's shoulder.

'At least this much is settled, that someone has made a copy of the key of the one-eyed beloved's father.'

'Ahan. But why?'

'That I will report to you after making inquiries.'

'Whom will you inquire from?'

'I will ask from the endless sky, the star-filled night, the slow-moving beauties...I mean, the breeze...'

Fayyaz didn't reply. Imran continued muttering, 'But it will be relatively easier to obtain the key of the mister martyr's grave keeper. We will have to find out the history of that building. I think we have reached its vicinity. Stop the bike.'

Fayyaz stopped the bike.

'Turn off the engine.'

Fayyaz turned off the engine. Imran took the bike from him and hid it behind a nearby bush.

'What do you want?' Fayyaz asked him.

'I want to know why you want me to tag along everywhere you go?' Imran said.

'That murder...it took place in this building.'

'Don't call it murder. Call it an accident.'

'Accident? What do you mean?'

'For meanings, please see Ghayyas's Dictionary, page one hundred and twelve. By the way, chapter hundred and twelve is also called Aikso Bara, which reminds me of the famous actress Begum Para. And with Begum Para the use of Amrit Dhara is necessary, otherwise you'll lose your hair like the famous actor David...'[1]

Fayyaz, deeply irritated, fell silent.

Both of them were slowly heading toward, the building. First they went around the entire building and then stopped in front of the main entrance.

'Oh!' Imran whispered. 'It's not locked.'

'How can you see? I cannot make out anything!'

'You are not an owl,' Imran said. 'Now move away from here.'

Both of them walked to the rear of the house. Imran looked up; the wall was quite high. He took out his torch and shone it over the wall.

'Will you be able to bear my weight?' he asked Fayyaz.

---

[1] This absurd-sounding statement is a word play on 'aikso bara', which is Urdu for hundred and twelve. Aikso bara is rhymed with (Amrit) Dhara which is then connected to (Begum) Para, a 1940s Bollywood actress. The reference to the actress is then used to connect with the actor David.

'I don't understand.'

'To make you understand one needs the whole paraphernalia of blackboards and chalks and sticks. I mean I want to go up.'

'Why? Do you think someone's in there?' Fayyaz asked.

'No. I just want to shoot the breeze. Now sit.'

'The wall will still be higher...'

'Yaar, please, don't make useless arguments,' Imran said, annoyed. 'Otherwise I am going back.'

Willingly or unwillingly, Fayyaz sat at the base of the wall.

'At least take off your shoes!' Fayyaz said.

'Don't run away with them,' Imran said, taking off his shoes. He then stood on Fayyaz's shoulders. 'Now stand.'

Fayyaz stood up slowly. Imran's hand reached the light vent and the next moment he was scaling the wall like a monkey. Fayyaz watched him, his jaw dropping. He didn't know if Imran was devil or man. Was he the same fool who sometimes looked as harmless as an insect?

Using the same light vent with the help of which he had climbed up, Imran descended to the other side. Leaning against the wall, he waited for a few moments and then slowly moved towards the area from where he could hear footsteps. He could make out that there were men in the room where he had seen the murdered corpse. The door of the room was closed but a faint candlelight escaped the edges of the door. Everything else was in complete darkness.

With his back against the wall, Imran proceeded cautiously towards the door. Suddenly his eyes were drawn to the martyr's tomb: its tombstone was rising and there was a faint light coming from the space between the tombstone and the ground. Two frightening eyes stared out from the space into the darkness.

Imran stopped short in his tracks, wide-eyed at this sight. Then a deafening shriek came out of the tomb. It sounded like a scream from a monkey caught between a dog's jaws. Imran quickly slipped into the next room. He knew what effect this cry would have on the others in the room. He stood near the door, keeping his eyes on the tomb. The tombstone was still raised and the eyes peering out burnt like sparks of fire. Another cry rose in the air and the door flung open. There was one more cry, but this was different from the others because it was from one of the unidentified men. 'G-g-g...Ghost!' someone said in a trembling voice. And then it felt as if a few men were rushing for the main door.

In a little while, everything became quiet and the tombstone returned to its original position.

Crawling with his chest to the ground, Imran also headed towards the main door. He turned a couple of times to look at the tomb but the tombstone did not move any more.

After satisfying himself that the main door was locked from the outside, Imran returned.

The door of the room with the murdered corpse was open. But now darkness reigned supreme in there. Imran carefully closed the door and took out his torch. He was shocked at what he saw by its light. '*Inna lillahi wa' inna illai'hi raaji'un,*' Imran muttered slowly. 'May God have mercy on you too.'

At the place where he had last seen a murdered body, lay another one. On his back were also three wounds from which blood had spilled on the ground. This was quite a handsome youth, and judging from his dress, he seemed upper class.

'Today's their turn, tomorrow's ours...' Imran muttered in his dervish-like tone. He held a piece of paper in his hand, which he had taken out from the young man's tight clasp with some difficulty. Using his torch, Imran examined the corpse for some time, and then with a meaningful nod, he hid the paper in the inside pocket of his coat. The rest of the rooms looked in the same condition as before. There was no apparent change.

Soon he was descending through the same vent he had used to enter the building. He stepped on the last vent and hopped down.

'I've only just discovered this speciality of yours,' Fayyaz said, looking at Imran in amazement. He smiled and added, 'Did you meet a she-monkey in there?'

'Did the cry reach you here?' Imran asked.

'Yes. But I have not seen monkeys around this area.'

'Did you hear anything else?'

'Yes. Probably you cried out of fear?' Fayyaz asked.

'You want the murdered body now or in the morning?'

'Murdered body!' Fayyaz jumped. 'What nonsense! What body?'

'With this murder, the poet has produced his second ghazal in the same series.'

'O you smartest of fools, state clearly what you mean,' Fayyaz said in an irritated tone.

'Another body. Three wounds with the same five inches between them. The postmortem too will prove the depth of these wounds to be equal.'

'Yaar, please, don't fool around with me,' Fayyaz said, exhausted by Imran's ramblings.

'You have the Judge sahib's key, you be the smart one,' Imran said dryly.

'But how did this happen?'

'In the same way poetry happens. But this particular instance looks to me like an artificially contrived poem. Like this couplet by Mir:

O what do you ask about
Creed of 'Mir'? well, he has put Mark on his
brow, sat in fane
Gave up Islam long ago.

Now tell me why he feigned sitting, and did not sit in reality?'

'Oh it is not feign, it is fane, meaning a temple...' Fayyaz said and then regained his senses. 'Oh my God. Why am I getting tangled up in these lexical debates? That body? Where is it?'

'In that same room, in that very same spot where we found the first body.'

'But what were those cries about?' Fayyaz asked.

'It would be better if you don't ask about them. I have not seen a more ridiculous sight in my life.'

'Meaning?'

35

'First I saw a donkey on which a she-monkey was riding. Then I saw another shadow, which was certainly of a man. In the darkness, I think it is possible to distinguish between a donkey and a man. What do you think?'

'I feel sad that you are always so unserious.'

'Yaar, Fayyaz! Tell me honestly: if you see a man kissing a she-monkey, will you laugh or feel angry?'

'You are wasting my time.'

'All right, let's go.' Imran tapped on his shoulder. Both of them reached the main door.

'Why are you being a pain?' Fayyaz said.

'Take out the key.'

Opening the door, they reached the room with the body. Imran switched on his torch, but the next instant he was stroking his head as though it had suddenly become hot.

The body had disappeared.

'What kind of a joke is this?' Fayyaz turned to him angrily.

'Good poets often take out weak lines from their poems.'

'Yaar, Imran, I think I have had enough of your help.'

'But my dear, look here, as the verse goes:
the image is a plaintiff—about whose mischievousness of writing?—the one who disappeared with the body couldn't do anything about the fresh blood stains.
O my assassin, make an example of my murder
So that no one loves another ever again...'

Fayyaz jumped to examine the bloodstains on the ground. 'But what happened to the body?' he asked in a confused voice.

'Angels lifted it to heavens. The murdered was a *bihishti*. Oh, but that is also the word for a water supplier. Oh, what will you call it? My head's spinning. I will get a stroke. '

'*Bihishti* means destined for paradise. That's what we'll say. God will deal with you, Imran.'

'*Jiyo*. Yes, the dead man was destined for paradise. So what was I saying?'

'Why didn't you stay here?' Fayyaz said, upset. 'You should have just called out to me.'

'Listen, my friend! Forget a she-monkey, I have never kissed a housefly...' Imran said in a disappointed tone.

'What is the matter? You have referred to a she-monkey several times...'

'What I've just told you is absolutely correct. That man took the she-monkey off the back of the donkey, took it into the room, and then the she-monkey shouted and that man...then there was silence. Then I saw the corpse. The donkey and the monkey had disappeared.'

'Are you reporting correctly?' Fayyaz said in a hoarse voice.

'Whoever considers me a liar may face the wrath of God.'

Fayyaz thought for a moment and then said in a frightened voice, 'Then...then...I think...we should leave it till morning...'

Imran's glance paused at the tomb. The tombstone

was raised and those dreadful eyes were staring into the darkness again. Imran turned off the torch and pushed Fayyaz behind the wall. He didn't want Fayyaz to see that spectacle.

'Wha...What...' Fayyaz said, trembling.

'The she-monkey,' Imran said. He was about to say something more, but the shriek filled the air once more.

'Aray...baap!' Fayyaz exclaimed like a frightened child.

'Close your eyes,' Imran instructed him in all seriousness. 'Seeing such things can cause heart failures. Have you brought your revolver?'

'No. No. Did you ask me to?'

'That's okay...Now wait...' Imran said, slowly moving towards the door.

The tombstone was now level again and the silence suddenly felt much deeper to them.

'Get ready,' Imran turned to him.

'For...For what?'

'The she-monkey is riding the donkey.'

'Then?' Fayyaz said, wetting his dry lips.

'You pick up the monkey, I will get on the donkey.'

'Yaar, please. Don't frighten me further. This place is haunted.'

'Okay. Then you get on the donkey. It's the same thing.'

Imran could feel Fayyaz's heart thud.

'Come on! Let's get out of here, ' Imran said, taking hold of his hand and dragging him out.

'But…?'

'Let's go. I'm scared!' Imran said.

'But that…'

'Oh, come on now!' Imran pushed him towards the door.

Fayyaz was not walking but dragging himself towards the door. Somehow they got out. After closing the door, they locked it. For the rest of the way, Imran went on explaining to Fayyaz that turning back in such situations was like inviting sickness upon oneself.

Chapter 5

IT WAS ONE AM. Fayyaz sped off after dropping off Imran near his house.

The gate in front of his house was closed. Imran shook the door. The guard, who had dozed off, cried out with a start.

'Guard, my dear, I am your menial servant, Ali Imran, MSc, PhD, London.'

'Who? Oh, the young master!' He came near the gate. 'Sir, it's difficult.'

'All great men have repeated over and again that there is no difficulty which cannot be overcome.'

'The master has ordered that the gate may not be opened. Please tell me what to do.'

'All right. Then please convey Confucius's message to your master.'

'Yes, young master?' the guard said, a little puzzled.

'Tell him that Confucius says open your doors for the honest people lost in night's darkness.'

'But the master said...'

'Ha! The master! He should have born in China. Anyway, please convey Confucius's message to him.'

'What should I tell him?' the guard asked in a trembling voice. 'Where will you go now?'

'This fakir will spend the night in some graveyard.'

'Can I do something for you?'

'Yes. Pray for my forgiveness. Okay. Ta ta.' Imran walked off.

Half an hour later, he entered Tip Top Nightclub. At the door, however, he ran into the Deputy Director of the Intelligence Bureau who had also been his father's class fellow.

'So, young man. So now you have also started frequenting these places?'

'Yes. I often come by to play Flush,' Imran said respectfully.

'Flush! Oh, so now you play Flush as...'

'Yes, yes. I feel like it when I am a bit drunk...'

'Oh! So you have also started drinking?'

'What can I say? I swear I've never drunk alone. Frequently I find hookers who do not agree to anything without a drink...'

'Oh, my Lord! So you are ruining your father's name?'

'Please tell me,' Imran said in a despondent tone, 'what should I do when I can't find a girl from a good family? By the way, I promise, the moment I find a nice girl I will curse the hookers and thank the Lord...'

The Deputy Director stared at him for a while and then said, 'I think Rahman sahib doesn't know, but I guess...'

'If you meet him, please relate this particular Confucian proverb to him: When an honest man doesn't find refuge in his own house, he turns to dark alleys and has dealings with the barking dogs therein.'

The Deputy Director was left staring at him.

Imran puckered his lips as if he were whistling and scanned the hall in front of him. His eyes paused at a table where a beautiful woman was smoking a cigarette with a bottle of port wine in front of her. Her glass was more than half empty. Imran stopped in front of her.

'Can I sit here, Lady Jehangir?' he said, bowing a little.

'Oh you!' Lady Jehangir said, lifting her right brow. 'No. Absolutely not.'

'No worries,' he said, sitting down. 'Confucius advised me to.'

'I have no interest in Confucius,' she said shortly.

'All right. Then listen to a line from D.H. Lawrence...'

'I don't want to hear a thing. Go away from here,' said Lady Jehangir, lifting her glass of wine.

'At least have some consideration. You were once my fiancée.'

'Shut up.'

'Suit yourself. I just wanted to tell you that the weather was particularly pleasant this morning.'

She broke into a smile.

'Sit down,' she said and emptied her glass in a swig. She fixed her intoxicated eyes on his face and, taking a long drag of her cigarette, leaned toward him and said quietly, 'I'm still yours.'

'But...Sir Jehangir?' Imran said.

'Oh, bury him already...'

'Hain? Is he dead?' Imran asked confusedly, standing up.

Lady Jehangir laughed.

'Your antics are so endearing,' she said, winking at him. Imran bent his head coyly.

'What would you like to drink?' Lady Jahangir asked.

'Lassi.'

'Lassi?' Lady Jahangir giggled. 'You must be drunk!'

'No, wait!' Imran was startled. 'After one in the afternoon I just take coffee... Then from six in the evening till midnight I just have rum.'

'Rum?' Lady Jehangir made a face. 'You are not in my league; rum is for peasants.'

'When drunk, I forget that I am from the rural areas.'

'What are you doing these days?'

'Forbearing and persevering,' Imran said, heaving a deep sigh.

'Can't you be serious about any part of your life?' Lady Jehangir asked him, smiling.

'Oh...so you think so too?' Imran's voice sounded pained now.

'Why did you refuse to marry me?' Lady Jehangir said.

'When did I refuse?' Imran said with an impish look on his face. 'I only recited a few poems to your respected father. How was I supposed to know that

43

he had no interest in poetry; otherwise I would have restricted myself to prose.'

'In my father's opinion you are utterly uncouth and a fool,' she said.

'And since Sir Jehangir is of the same age as your father, therefore...'

'Shut up!' Lady Jehangir said angrily.

'Nevertheless, I will die suffering like this,' Imran said, mournful again.

Lady Jehangir was studying his face carefully.

'Do you really regret that decision of yours?' she asked in a low voice.

'*You* ask me this? And that too as if you doubt me...' Imran's eyes quickly filled with tears, which even started falling down his face.

'Arrr...no, no, my dear...Imran darling... What are you doing?' She passed across her handkerchief.

'I will die of this grief,' Imran said, wiping off his tears.

'No. You should get married,' Lady Jehangir said. 'As for me, I'll always be yours.' She was filling a second glass of wine.

'Everyone says this. There have been a few marriage proposals as well. A few days back, there was an offer from Justice Faruqi's daughter as well. My parents refused. But I somewhat liked that offer.'

'Liked it?' Lady Jehangir said, surprised. 'Have you seen the girl?'

'Yes. That one, right, who has a Rita Hayworth hairstyle and usually wears dark specs?'

'You know why she wears those specs?'

'No. But she looks good in them.'

Lady Jehangir laughed out loudly. 'She wears those glasses because she's blind in one eye.'

'Hain?' Imran jumped.

'And probably that is the reason your family did not accept the proposal.'

'Do you know her?' Imran asked.

'Very well. And these days I see her with a handsome man. Quite possibly he's an idiot like you.'

'Who is he? I will break his neck!' Imran roared. Then with a start, he muttered to himself, '*La haula wala quwwat!* What do I care?'

'It is very surprising to see such a handsome young man court a one-eyed girl...'

'Truly. He must be the eighth wonder of the world,' said Imran. 'Do I know him?'

'I don't know. At least I don't know him and, if I don't know him, he cannot be from an aristocratic family of this city.'

'How long have you been seeing them together?'

'For some fifteen–twenty days.'

'Do they come here as well?'

'No. But I have seen them in Café Camino quite often.'

'Ah. Mirza Ghalib was right when he said:
A lament, the wealth of a whole world; and the
world, a handful of dust the sky appears as the
egg of a turtledove, to me.'

'What does that mean?' Lady Jehangir asked.

'I don't know,' Imran replied innocently and began drumming with his fingers on the table.

'There will certainly be some rain before morning,' Lady Jehangir said, stretching.

'I don't see Sir Jehangir around these days,' Imran said.

'He's out of the country for a month.'

'Good!' Imran smiled.

'Why?' Lady Jehangir looked at him meaningfully.

'Nothing. Confucius has said...'

'Stop being such a bore, Imran.'

'By the way, do you plan to stay here the whole night?'

'No. Not really. Why?'

'I want to sit alone somewhere and cry.'

'You are a complete ass. In fact, worse than an ass...'

'I think so too. Will you give me the opportunity to cry under your roof? Confucius has said...'

'Imran! Please. Shut up!'

'Lady Jehangir, I am as sad as a lifeless cockerel.'

'Okay. Get up. But leave your Confucius here. I cannot stand this boring talk.'

About half an hour later, Imran stood in Lady Jehangir's bedroom and was looking at her goggle-eyed. Lady Jehangir was wearing only a nightgown. She stretched her arms and smiled at him. 'What are you thinking?' she asked in a voice brimming with suggestion.

'I am thinking why the sum of three angles of a triangle is equal to the sum of two right angles.'

'You have started your nonsense again?' There was some annoyance in Lady Jehangir's intoxicated eyes.

'My dear Lady Jehangir, if I prove that there is nothing called a right angle, I can become a celebrity.'

'You can go to hell,' Lady Jehangir murmured, making a face.

'Hell? Do you believe in hell?'

'Imran! I am going to kick you out!'

'Lady Jehangir, I am feeling sleepy.'

'In Sir Jehangir's bedroom you'll find his sleeping suit. Wear that.'

'Thank you. Which way is his bedroom?'

'The room in front of you,' she said and began pacing anxiously up and down her room.

Imran entered the connecting room and locked it from the inside. Lady Jehangir went on walking anxiously. Ten minutes elapsed. Eventually, she came to the door and pushed to open it—but it had been latched.

'What are you doing, Imran?' She started thumping the door, but did not get a response. She thought that she could hear Imran was snoring. She put her ear to the door; they were actually snoring sounds.

The next moment she was standing on a chair, looking through the glass panel above the door. She saw Imran lying on Sir Jehangir's bed with his shoes on. He had not even bothered to turn off the lights. She pursed her lips, staring at Imran like a hungry cat, and then hit the glass and broke it. The servants were perhaps sleeping in their quarters; otherwise the noise of the shattered glass would have certainly woken at least one of them. The noise, of course, did not disturb Imran in the least.

Lady Jehangir put her hand through the broken glass and dropped the latch. She was drunk and had put all her weight on the door. The moment the latch dropped, the door flung open and she tumbled into the bedroom along with her chair.

'Yes, yes. Synthetic gas smells a bit sweet,' Imran uttered in a drowsy voice and turned in his sleep. God knows if he was really awake or just muttering in his sleep.

Lady Jehangir, meanwhile, was on the floor, rubbing her forehead. After a couple of minutes, she got up and started hitting Imran. 'You swine! Scoundrel! Is this your father's house? Get up and get out of here!' She shook him violently. Imran sat up with a start.

'Hain? Has everyone run away?'

'Get lost from here!' Lady Jehangir pulled his collar.

'Okay, okay. Everything's all right.' Imran freed his collar and fell back again.

This time she seized him by his hair and made him stand up.

'Hain? Has he not left yet?' Imran sat up irritated. There was a full-sized mirror in front of him.

'Oh, so it is you!' he exclaimed, looking at his own reflection. He made a fist as if to attack the person in the mirror. Then, he slowly started advancing towards the mirror, cautiously measuring steps as if to confront an enemy. And then he moved away from the mirror and began walking along the edge of the room. When he approached the mirror, he stood against the wall. He looked at lady Jehangir and put a finger to his lips as though he was standing not next to a mirror but a door—lying in wait to attack an enemy entering through the door. Lady Jehangir looked at him incredulously. Before she could utter a word, he turned around and punched the mirror. As soon as his hand hit the mirror, he seemed to wake up from his slumber.

'Oh, my God!' he said, rubbing his eyes. Then he began to giggle. Seeing this, Lady Jehangir also started laughing, but she grew serious again.

'Why did you come here?'

'Oh! I think I forgot. Maybe I was sad. Lady Jehangir, you are very kind. I want to cry.'

'Go cry on your father's grave. Get out of here!'

'Lady Jehangir! Confucius...'

'Shut up!' Lady Jehangir snarled.

'Okay, all right.' Imran said obediently, nodding his head as though she had gently advised him to shut up.

'Get out of here!'

'Very well!' Imran said obediently. He then walked out of the room and entered Lady Jehangir's bedroom. He was about to sit on her bed when Lady Jehangir stormed into the room.

'Now I will have to wake up the servants,' she said.

'Oh, please. You shouldn't bother. I will go and wake them up. Do you need them for something important?'

'Imran, I'll kill you!' Lady Jehangir shouted.

'But please don't tell anyone about it...otherwise the police...well, I am ready to die anyway. Would you like me sharpen any knives for the occasion? If you are planning to use a revolver, I would not advise that. The sound can be heard at quite a distance in the silence. Poison would be ideal.'

'Imran, for God's sake!' she said desperately.

'God's a far cry! I can give my life for the meanest of his servants as well! Whatever my love desires!'

'*What* is it that you want?' she enquired.

'One of the two things...'

'What?'

'Death or two hours of sleep.'

'I didn't know you were such an ass.'

'If you had asked me I could have told you much earlier.'

'Go to hell,' she said and left the room, showering him with abuses. Imran got up and closed the door. He took off his shoes and got into bed with his clothes on.

Chapter 6

IT WOULD BE ENTIRELY incorrect to think that Imran had headed to the Tip Top Nightclub without any reason. He had already known that Sir Jehangir was not in town and he also knew where Lady Jehangir spent her nights on such occasions. It was also true that Lady Jehangir, at one point in time, had been his fiancée, but their marriage had been called off because of Imran's foolishness. Sir Jehangir's age was certainly around sixty, but he did not look very old because of his strong build.

Imran lay still on the bed. Half an hour passed. He glanced at his wristwatch, then got up from the bed and turned off the light. He tiptoed to the connecting door, which was locked from the other side. A dark blue light was visble and Imran peeped inside from the glass of the door. Lady Jehangir was fast asleep, lying on her belly. Her well-built fox terrier was resting its head on her waist and was fast asleep too.

Imran entered Sir Jehangir's library as cautiously as before.

It was dark in there. Imran took out a torch from his pocket and turned it on. It was quite a large room. There were huge shelves on all four sides and there were three large tables in the centre of the room.

It looked more like a public reading room than a private library.

On the east side of the room, there was a writing desk. Imran headed for it. He took out the paper that he had found near the corpse in that haunted building, examined it for a moment, and then began to sift through the papers on the desk.

He was astonished when he saw the letterhead of the writing pad on the desk. There was no difference between the stamp on the piece of paper in his hand and the one on the letterhead; both were exactly the same. This stamp was the family insignia of Sir Jehangir's ancestors and their services during the Mughal period. Sir Jehangir was still using this stamp. His stationery usually had the stamp printed on them instead of his name.

Imran rearranged the papers in their original order and left the library. According to Lady Jehangir, Sir Jehangir was not here for a month. Then how come...?

Imran's mind was galloping: after all, what relation did these events have with Sir Jehangir? Before returning to the bedroom, he peeped again into the room where Lady Jehangir was sleeping and, with a smile, he returned to the room where he had been lying down.

At nine o'clock in the morning, Lady Jehangir was shaking him violently, trying to wake him up.

'Well done! Well done!' Imran sprang up, bewildered. He sat stiffly on the edge of the bed and began clapping as if cheering players in a stadium.

'What nonsense is this?' Lady Jehangir said, annoyed.

'Oh! Sorry!' He gave a start and then looked at her with a puzzled expression. 'Hello, Lady Jehangir! So tell me, why did you take the trouble of coming here so early in the morning?'

'Have you lost your mind?' Lady Jehangir said in an acerbic tone.

'Quite possibly,' Imran made a face and then starting calling out the names of his servants.

Lady Jehangir stared at him for a few moments and then said, 'Please, it will be better if you leave now. Otherwise...'

'Hain? Who are you to tell me to leave my own house?' Imran jumped up to his feet.

'You think this is your father's house?' Lady Jehangir's voice rose.

Imran looked around at the walls of the room and then suddenly jumped up and said, 'Aray! Where am I? This doesn't seem to be my room!'

'Now leave before I call in my servants...'

'Why do you need the servants? Can I do something for you? By the way, you look beautiful when you're angry...'

'Shut up.'

'All right. I will not say a word.' Imran made a face. Then he sat back on the bed.

Lady Jehangir was looking at him as if she was ready to tear him apart. She was out of breath now and her face was flushed. Imran slipped on his shoes, took his coat off the hook and then stopped in front of Lady Jehangir's dressing table, combing his hair and humming a song as if it was his own table. Lady Jehangir was seething with anger.

'Ta ta.' Imran turned to look at her when he reached the door and then exited, smiling like a fool. His mind was clear now. Last night's information was enough to satisfy him. That a page from Sir Jehangir's letter pad indicated that there was some link between Sir Jehangir and the murdered man. Perhaps Jehangir was in the city. And perhaps Lady Jehangir did not know this.

Now Imran was concerned about the good-looking man who had been seen with the judge's daughter.

'We'll see!' he muttered quietly to himself.

He had no desire to return home, but he was compelled to do so. How else would he get the bike? He also had to find out who had originally owned that haunted building. If the building's owner was a stranger to the villagers, then it was conceivable that the owner did not build it himself but bought it because its construction style was pretty old.

At his house, misfortune awaited him. His mother was waiting for him, full of anger. She became furious the moment she saw him. 'Where were you, you scoundrel! Swine!'

'Oho...Amma bi...Good morning...Dearest...'

'Morning? Where the hell were you last night?'

'Oh Amma, what do I tell you. You know Hazrat Maulana...in fact, you know our spiritual saint, Hazrat Maulana Syedna Jigar Muradabadi, right? I presented myself before Maulvi Tafazzul Husain last night. Oh Lord, what a saint...I think I will start praying regularly from today...'

'You scoundrel. You are trying to fool me,' said the old lady with a frustrated smile.

'God forgive me, Amma bi!' Imran started wailing. 'My paradise is beneath your feet.'[1]

Surayya approached them and Imran wanted to slip away. The old woman kept on muttering.

'Amma bi you are ruining your health for no reason,' Surayya said, coming closer. 'There is no point in arguing with him. Let Imran bhai be. Only God will ask him to account for his deeds...'

Imran didn't say anything. But he couldn't leave Amma bi muttering with anger.

'You don't have any shame, do you? Bringing disgrace to your father's good name, knocking around his turban...'[2] Surayya said.

'Hain? So has Abba jan started wearing turbans now?' Imran cried out joyfully.

Amma bi suffered from palpitation and tachycardia, and had weak nerves. She was often enraged and in such situations her hand naturally moved towards the slipper. Soon Imran could hear nothing but tara-tar, the sound of the slipper hitting him. After Amma bi was done beating him, she broke down and started crying. Surayya pulled her into another

---

[1] A reference to the Islamic saying, 'Paradise is at the feet of your mother,' meaning if you take care of her, your place in paradise is assured.

[2] *Pagri uchhalna*: to disgrace, to dishonour.

room. Imran's three cousins, Zarina, Mumtaz, and Soofia immediately surrounded him. One began to brush the dust off his coat, another corrected the knot of his tie. The third started giving him a head massage.

Imran took out the cigarette from his coat pocket, lit it up, and behaved as if he was completely alone. After taking a few drags, he headed for his room, leaving his cousins puzzled. In his room, Imran tossed his felt hat in one direction, flung the coat on the bed, and dozed off on a comfortable chair.

The piece of paper he found last night was still in his hand. Some numbers were written on it, some measurements. It seemed as if a carpenter, before setting out to make something, had made estimations. The paper seemed to have no value, yet it did have some relation to the dead man's body; to the man murdered in mysterious circumstances—and it was the second murder in an identical manner.

Imran had no knowledge of the investigations of the police or the Intelligence Bureau with regard to the murders. He didn't even bother checking with Fayyaz about the analysis of the police.

Imran put the paper in his suitcase and, changing into a new suit, got ready to leave again. Soon his bike approached the village of the haunted building. He had no difficulty in finding out who the building's original owner was.

He met a respectable person from the family of the man who had sold the building to Judge sahib's friend. 'This was some eight years ago,' he told him.

'Ayaz sahib bought that building from us. Afterwards, just before he died, he transferred it legally to some Judge sahib.'

'Who was Ayaz sahib? Where did he live before buying this building?' Imran questioned.

'We don't know. He lived here for about three years after buying the building but no one knows who he was or where he lived before this. He had a servant with him who now lives in the front part of the building.'

'That keeper of the grave?' Imran said, and the old man nodded his head in agreement. The man thought for a while and then said, 'Ayaz sahib discovered that grave. Our family did not know about it. There was no grave there before. We did not hear about it from our ancestors either.'

'Oh!' Imran said, staring at him. 'So how was the grave discovered?'

'He had a dream that there was a saint buried there. He started building the grave the next day.'

'He started building it himself?'

'Yes. He did all his work by himself. He was quite a wealthy man as well, but you cannot say he was stingy because he was quite generous when giving out alms.'

'The walls of the room in which we found the body are plastered; the rest of the rooms are not. What is the reason for this?'

'Ayaz sahib plastered the room himself.'

'Himself?'

'Yes.'

'There must be some gossip about this here in the village?'

'Absolutely not, sir. People think that Ayaz sahib was an exalted saint, and I personally think that his servant is not without holiness as well.'

'Did Ayaz sahib receive any visitors who were strangers to the people of this village?'

'No. I don't remember any such people. I think no visitor ever came to see him.'

'Okay. Thank you very much.' Imran shook hands with the old man and turned towards his bike.

Imran headed to the building with his mind brewing with questions. Ayaz had made that grave himself and even plastered the room himself. Was he a good architect as well? The grave wasn't there before. It was Ayaz's discovery and his servant was still stuck to the grave. But why? And why was this particular room plastered?

Imran reached the building. The keeper of the grave lived in a small room just outside the building. The room was open and the keeper was present. Imran looked at him carefully: he was a powerfully built, middle-aged man, with a dense beard and red eyes—which perhaps always remained that way.

Imran blinked his eyes a few times and the foolish expression reappeared on his face.

'What's the matter?' the grave keeper called out, looking at him.

'I have found a job due to your prayers,' Imran said in a deferential tone. 'I thought I should pay you my respects.'

'Go away!' the grave keeper said, glaring at Imran with his bloodshot eyes.

'Please don't make me suffer this way.' Imran joined his hand pleadingly. 'I will make one last request.'

'Who are you? What do you want?' The keeper suddenly grew soft.

'Boy! Just one boy! Without a boy, my house feels lonely. O Holiness! I have had the yearning for a child for thirty years now!'

'Thirty years! What is your age now?' The guardian stared at him.

'Twenty five.'

'Get lost! You mock me. I will destroy you this very moment.'

'You are mistaken, O Holiness! I was asking for my father. He is getting married a second time.'

'Are you going or should I...!' the keeper said, getting up.

'My lord!' Imran said, joining his hands pleadingly. 'The police are about to trouble you.'

'Get lost. Policemen are asses. What will they do to a fakir?'

'There have been two murders under the fakir's shadow...'

'So what? Why doesn't the police ask the Judge sahib's daughter? Why did she come here? She came here with a young man.'

'O Holiness! The police really are a herd of donkeys. Please guide us.'

'Are you from the secret police?'

'No, my lord. I am a news reporter. If I get some news, it will help me get a meal...'

'Yes. Okay, sit down. I cannot tolerate that this house, which is the site of a saint's shrine, turns into a place for sinning. The police should do something to stop it.'

'O Holiness, I don't understand at all,' Imran said, looking disappointed.

'I will explain,' said the guardian of the grave, dilating his bloodshot eyes. 'On the fourteenth, Judge sahib's girl brought a friend of hers here and stayed inside for hours.'

'Didn't you object to it? If I were you, I would have smashed their heads. Goodness gracious! On a shrine of such a holy saint!' Imran started slapping his face.

'What could I do? It was like sipping poison. My master gave his house to them. Otherwise I would have taught them a lesson.'

'Your master?'

'Yes! Hazrat Ayaz Rahmatallah Ala'ih. He was my spiritual master. He has given me this room of the building so that I can take care of the shrine.'

'Where is Ayaz sahib's shrine?'

'In the graveyard. His will was that his grave be levelled so that it cannot be identified.'

'So do you recognize Judge sahib's daughter?'

'Yes, I know her. She's blind in one eye.'

'Hai!' Imran slapped his chest. The keeper stared at him.

'Okay, my lord. So she came here on the night of the fourteenth and this body was found here on the morning of the sixteenth.'

'Not one, now there will be thousands of these bodies!' the keeper said angrily. 'Disgrace has been brought upon the shrine!'

'But my lord, it is possible that the boy was her brother?'

'Not at all. Judge sahib does not have a son.'

'Then the matter...hip...' Imran said, scratching his right cheek.

Imran left the building and returned to the village. He questioned people for two–three hours and then set out for the city.

Chapter 7

CAPTAIN FAYYAZ WAS BUSY at work when Imran's message reached him. He had asked him to come to a restaurant near his office.

Fayyaz did not delay. Imran was sitting alone rapping his fingers on the table like a tabla player. Seeing Fayyaz, he smiled like a fool.

'Any new discoveries?' Fayyaz asked, taking a seat near him.

'Ghalib was actually Mir Taqi Mir's *nom de plume*.'

'You could have sent me this information through the post as well,' Fayyaz said peevishly.

'Where was my one-eyed beloved on the night of the fourteenth?'

'Why are you after her?'

'Find out and tell me. If she tells you she spent the night with one of her maternal aunts, then it is your duty to check this with her aunt and inform Hamdard Pharmacy, otherwise the exchange of letters will not be kept confidential.'

'Imran, I am very busy.'

'I can see that. Do you have lots of flies in your office to keep you busy? And by lots of flies I don't mean that they are performing gymnastics there.'

'I am leaving,' Fayyaz said, irritated, and got up to go.

'Don't the flies sit on your nose?' Imran said, catching hold of his hand and pulling him back to the seat.

Fayyaz sat down staring at him. He was really annoyed. 'Why did you come here?' he asked.

'Oh! I don't even remember now. I think I came here to ask you the going rate of rice. But now you will say that you are not a dancing girl and cannot tell me the rates. By the way, I can give you the news that so far as the murders are concerned, the hand of the one-eyed beloved is discernible. I haven't spoken a wrong word, have I?'

'Her hand? How?' Fayyaz was startled.

'This is what is written in the encyclopaedia.' Imran shook his head. 'Just find out where she spent the night of the fourteenth.'

'Are you serious?'

'Uff! Fools are always serious men.'

'Okay, I will find out.'

'May your female partner live long! The second thing is that I want complete information on Judge sahib's friend, Ayaz: who was he, where was he born, his family, where do his relatives live, have all of them died or are some alive.'

'Why don't you have tea at my place in the evening?' Fayyaz said.

'And what about the tea for now?' Imran asked innocently.

Fayyaz laughed and ordered the waiter to bring tea. Imran rolled his eyes like an owl. After a while, he said, 'Are you going to make me meet Judge sahib?'

'Yes, I will speak to him about it in your presence.'

'Hehehe...I will feel very shy,' Imran said, pressing his finger to his teeth.

'What's there to feel shy about?'

'No, I will send my respected father.'

'What nonsense are you talking?'

'I don't want to talk about my own marriage directly.'

'May God help me! I was talking about Ayaz!'

'*La haula wala quwwat!*' Imran said, acting embarrassed.

'Imran, act like a human, please.'

'All right,' Imran said, nodding his head obediently.

Tea was served. Fayyaz was distracted. Intermittently, he glanced at Imran who was making faces in the mirror hung on the opposite wall. Fayyaz poured tea for him and pushed forward the teacup.

Imran said, 'Yaar, Fayyaz, that keeper of the grave seems like a very great man.'

'Why?'

'Because he said such a great thing.'

'What?'

'That policemen are asses.'

'Why did he say this?' Fayyaz said with a start.

'I don't know. But he said something quite valuable.'

'Why are you abusing me needlessly?'

64

'No, my dear. All right, tell me who constructed the grave and what do you think of the plaster in that one room?'

'I don't waste my energy on nonsense,' Fayyaz said peevishly. 'How is this connected to the matter at hand?'

'Then the body of the murdered man isn't significant either,' Imran said.

'What are you getting at?' Fayyaz said impatiently.

'This: that good children greet their elders when they get up in the morning, then wash their faces and have breakfast, and then go to school. And in the school they open the textbooks and read: A for Apple, B for Bat, C for Cat...'

'Imran! For God's sake!' Fayyaz said, raising his hands.

'And they always remember God as well.'

'Go on with this nonsense.'

'All right, so I will turn silent. A single silence tancels a chousand talamities... Hain? What is talamities? *La haula wala quwwat!* What did I say just now?'

'Your head!'

'Yes. Thank you. I have a very strong head. Once it became so strong that I started calling it baigan ka bharta!'

'Finish your tea and get lost,' Fayyaz said. 'I have a lot of work now. Come to my house in the evening.'

Chapter 8

THAT EVENING IMRAN AND Fayyaz were sitting in Judge sahib's drawing room waiting for him. His daughter was also present. She was wearing her dark glasses. Imran looked at her again and again, heaving sighs. Fayyaz also stole glances at her.

Judge sahib came in and Rabia got up and left.

'I am sorry for bothering you,' Fayyaz said.

'No problem. Please go ahead.'

'Actually the thing is that I want more information about Ayaz.'

'I think I have already told you everything.'

'I want to know a few things about his family so that we can meet his relatives.'

'Sadly, I won't be able to tell you much in that respect,' Judge sahib said. 'It might seem strange to you, but it is true that I know nothing about him despite the fact we were close friends.'

'Can't you even tell us where he came from originally?'

'Sadly, I don't even know this much.'

'This is very strange. All right. Where did you first meet him?'

'England.'

Fayyaz was astonished at hearing this, but Imran sat impassively.

'When was this?' Fayyaz asked.

'Some thirty years ago—and this meeting took place in very strange circumstances. I was studying Law at Oxford. Once I got involved in a fight with an Englishman because of a misunderstanding. London thirty years ago was full of hatred. Extreme hatred. You can get an idea from the fact that outside a hotel there was a signboard that said, "Indians and dogs are not allowed." I cannot say if that board is still there but anyway, in such an environment, the outcome was obvious if there was ever a misunderstanding between an Indian and an Englishman. It was at a restaurant. This was the East End of London where men were quite wild. Even today, this area is inhabited by the same kind of people. Extremely uncivilized people who live like animals. Oh, I am prolonging this account for nothing. I just meant to say that the fight grew bigger. To tell you the truth, I just wanted get out of there alive. Suddenly a man tore through the crowd. It was Ayaz. That was the first time I met him. The crowd, which was ready to kill me, dispersed on seeing Ayaz. It was as if a wolf had barged into a flock of sheep. Later I discovered that Ayaz was among the most influential people of the area. Why this was, I could never find out. Our relationship grew, but I never managed to discover anything about his personal life. He was an Indian as well, but I couldn't even find out which province, which city he was from.'

Judge sahib fell silent and extended a cigar case to them. Imran sat quietly, staring at the ceiling.

It seemed as if Fayyaz had dragged in a fool. Not just any fool, but someone who seemed incapable of understanding the conversation. Fayyaz glanced at him several times from the corner of his eye, but he remained quiet.

'Thank you!' Fayyaz said, taking a cigar and then gestured towards Imran. 'He doesn't smoke.'

In spite of this, Imran did not take his eyes off the ceiling. Judge sahib looked at him curiously but did not say anything. Suddenly Imran sighed, 'Allah,' and sat up straight. Like a madman, he chewed his mouth while looking at both of them.

Fayyaz was relieved that the Judge sahib did not inquire about Imran. Fayyaz was thinking up another question and hoping that Imran would stay quiet. But maybe Imran was an expert face reader as well, because he started talking the next moment. 'Yes sir, good people have short lives. Ayaz sahib was a saint of God. "When has the perverse and rough wheel of the Heavens spared someone..." as Ghalib's verse goes...'

But before Imran could complete the verse, Fayyaz spoke up, 'Yes, there is such a rumour among the villagers.'

'Bhai, I cannot swallow this rumour. I have heard it as well,' Judge sahib said. 'After his death I met some respectable people of the village; even they thought he was some exalted saint. But I don't think so. He had a mysterious personality but not in that way.'

'What do you think of the servant who takes care of the grave?' Fayyaz asked.

68

'He too is an exalted saint!' Imran interjected. Judge sahib stared at him but still did not ask anything about him.

'Was it mentioned in the will that the keeper of the grave would occupy and retain the outside room of the building?' Fayyaz asked Judge sahib.

'Yes, absolutely,' Judge sahib said sombrely. 'It would be better if we talk of something else. My relation to that building is limited to the fact that I am the legal owner of the building and nothing else. None of the members of my household has lived there.'

'Has no one ever visited it either?' Fayyaz asked.

'At the beginning everyone wanted to see it. Obviously, it came into our possession in a most strange manner.'

'There were showers of holy light on Ayaz sahib's funeral.' Imran threw in a comment again.

'I do not know,' Judge sahib said wearily. 'He was already buried when I reached the funeral.'

'I think that building is haunted,' Fayyaz said.

'Possibly. I wish it had not been my property. Will you gentlemen now excuse me?'

'We are sorry,' Fayyaz said, getting up. 'We have troubled you very much, but the situation is such.'

Fayyaz and Imran came out. Fayyaz was annoyed and as soon as they were out, he said angrily, 'You exhibit your stupidity everywhere.'

'And I am thinking I should shoot you,' Imran said.

'Why? What did I do?'

'Why didn't you ask him where was my one-eyed beloved on the night of the fourteenth?'

'Why are you pestering me? I am not in a good mood.'

'Anyway, I don't care. I will inquire about it myself,' Imran said. 'Do you know Sir Jehangir?'

'Yes, why?'

'He's my rival for my beloved.'

'So be it. What do I care?'

'Find out somehow where he is'

'Don't waste my time,' Fayyaz said, annoyed.

'Then you should go there where Satan will go on the Day of Judgement,' said Imran, and started walking swiftly towards Judge sahib's garage where Rabia was taking out her car.

'Miss Saleem.' Imran cleared his throat. 'I think we were introduced earlier.'

'Oh...yes, yes,' Rabia replied quickly.

'Can you give me a ride?'

'Please hop right in.'

Rabia was driving herself; Imran thanked her and sat next to her.

'Where do you want to be dropped off?' Rabia asked.

'The truth is, really, that I wouldn't want to get off.'

Rabia could only smile. She was wearing an artificial eye now and didn't have her dark glasses on. Fayyaz's wife had told her a lot about Imran, and so she was not ready to think of him as a fool.

'Are you upset with me?'

70

'Sorry?' Rabia was surprised. 'No,' she said and started laughing.

'I thought maybe it was so. Most people are usually upset with me. They say that I make them angry for nothing.'

'I don't know. So far you have not made me angry.'

'Then this is my good fortune,' Imran said. 'However, if I try I can make you angry.'

Rabia laughed again. 'Please do try.'

'So you think it is impossible?' Imran laughed like a fool.

'I don't ever get angry.'

'Okay then. Beware,' Imran said, as if he was a swordsman hollering out to another sword fighter in a cheap movie.

Rabia didn't say anything. She began to feel bored.

'Where were you on the night of the fourteenth?' Imran said suddenly.

'What?' Rabia was taken by surprise.

'Oh! Please mind the steering wheel lest we have an accident,' Imran said. 'See I made you angry.' Then he let out a loud laugh and slapped his thighs.

Rabia was out of breath and her hands on the steering wheel were trembling.

'Listen,' she said, panting. 'I want to return early. Where do you want to get off?'

'You have not answered my question,' Imran said calmly.

'Who are you to ask me?'

71

'See! You're angry. By the way, this is very important. If it reaches the police, there will be trouble. It is quite possible I could do something to make this question irrelevant to the police.'

Rabia did not say anything. She was licking her dry lips.

'I will not even ask where you were,' Imran said. 'Because I know. Just tell me who was with you?'

'I am feeling thirsty,' Rabia said in a weepy voice.

'Oho! So let's stop then. Café Nebraska is close by.'

A bit ahead, Rabia pulled over the car and both of them got off and entered Café Nebraska.

Imran chose an isolated corner and they sat down. Before ordering tea, Imran asked for a glass of cold water.

'I am certain you forgot the key behind with him.'

'With whom?' Rabia said incredulously.

'Don't worry. I am sure he had not even told you his correct name and address—and wouldn't have even met you after returning the key.'

Rabia was crestfallen. In a listless voice she said, 'Then what do you want to ask now?'

'When and how did you meet him?'

'Two months earlier.'

'Where?'

'At a party. I don't remember who introduced us.'

'Where was the party?'

'Perhaps it was the occasion of Sir Jehangir's birthday.'

'Oh!' Imran started thinking, then he said slowly. 'When did he return the key to you?'

'On the eve of the fifteenth.'

'And the body was discovered on the morning of the sixteenth,' Imran said.

Rabia started trembling. She replaced the teacup on the table and leaned back against the chair. She looked like a little bird caught in a falcon's claws.

'The key was with him all day on the fifteenth. He made a copy of it and returned it to you. And then he did not see you. Am I wrong?'

'That's right,' she said in a low voice. 'He told me he was a tourist staying at Jaafaria Hotel, but I went there the day before yesterday...'

She was quiet. Imran nodded his head, 'And there you discovered that a man with that name never stayed there.'

'Yes,' she said, lowering her head.

'He struck up this friendship only to get that key from you somehow.'

'I want to go home. I am not feeling well.'

'Just two minutes,' Imran said, waving his hand. 'Where did you meet him usually?'

'In Tip Top Nightclub.'

'How were his relations with Lady Jehangir?'

'Lady Jehangir?' she asked, irritated. 'Why are you bringing her up?'

'Will you not answer my question?' Imran asked politely.

'No. I don't think I have ever seen them with each other.'

'Thank you! Now I will not ask his name. Clearly, he wouldn't have told you his real name. But if you can tell me how he looked, I would be thankful.'

Rabia was compelled to explain. But she was distressed—and scared.

Chapter 9

IMRAN WAS STANDING ALONE on the footpath. Rabia had left. He took out a piece of chewing gum from his pocket and put it in his mouth, crushing it between his teeth. While thinking through things, chewing gum always proved to be his best friend. Unlike the detectives in mystery novels, he had no interest in cigars or pipes; he didn't even drink alcohol.

There were many questions in his mind and he stood on the corner of the footpath as if planning to cross the road. But the truth was he had no such intention.

He was thinking how Sir Jehangir could be linked to these matters. The piece of paper he had found near the second dead body was from Sir Jehangir's writing pad. Rabia had also met that mysterious man at Sir Jehangir's place; and the handsome young man Lady Jehangir mentioned could be no one else but this man. But then, Lady Jehangir did not know him. This much of what Lady Jehangir said was certainly true: that if this handsome man was really a member of an elite family of the city, she would have certainly known him. If Lady Jehangir was involved in some conspiracy, why mention it to Imran? It was possible she did not know about the dual life he led, but the question is, why mention it at all? This was not so important anyway. Hundreds of men were after girls, even if the girls were worse than junk. And then another question arose in his mind: why didn't that keeper of the grave tell the police about Rabia? He had stopped thinking about the grave and corpse. The worrying thing was who those people were and why they were so interested in the building. What was Sir Jehangir's connection with the building? Imran knew Sir Jehangir very well, but nothing about him seemed suspicious. He was among the city's most renowned and well-respected people.

After a while, Imran was getting ready to cross the road when a car screeched in front of him. It was Rabia.

'Thank God I found you,' she said, craning her head out of the window.

'I knew you'd need me,' Imran said, and opened the door and took the seat next to her.

'For God's sake, please save me,' Rabia said, trembling. 'I feel like I am drowning.'

'You consider me a straw for your support?'[1] Imran laughed out loudly.

'For God's sake, do something. If Daddy finds out about this...'

'It won't happen,' Imran replied seriously. 'I am happy that womenkind have come out into the open

---

[1] A reference to the Urdu phrase 'Doobtay ko tinkay ka sahara': The one who's sinking finds support even by clutching at straws.

to rub shoulders with your male counterparts. But you don't realize that men make an ulloo[2] out of you at every instance. By the way, what do we call the female of an ulloo?'

Rabia didn't reply and Imran went on, 'Anyway, forget about this. I will try and see to it that your name doesn't come up in this drama. Are you satisfied now? Stop the car...Okay. Ta ta!'

'Aray!' a little cry came out of Rabia's mouth as she floored the brakes.

'What happened?' Imran started to look around confusedly.

'It's *him*!' Rabia muttered. 'Get off. I will show him...'

'Who is it? What's the matter?'

'The guy who got me into this mess.'

'Where?'

'He has gone into that bar. He was the same guy. Leather jacket and beige pants.'

'Okay, you leave. I will take care of it.'

'No, I will also...'

'Leave!' Imran said with glowering eyes. Rabia suddenly felt scared. At that moment, that fool Imran actually looked frightening. She quietly turned the car.

Imran entered the bar. He saw the person instantly. He was sitting alone at a table: a well-built, graceful-

---

2 Ulloo literally means an owl in Urdu but it has negative connotations. It is commonly used to refer to a foolish person.

looking man. He had a broad forehead full of scars. Also he seemed to be in the habit of keeping his head tilted a little on the right. Imran sat at a table near him.

It looked as if the man was waiting for someone. He looked a little restless as well. Imran took out another piece of chewing gum and put it in his mouth. His guess was not far off the mark. A little while later a man entered the bar and sat next to the man wearing the leather jacket.

'It's turning into a mess,' the leather jacket man said.

'That old man has become neurotic,' the other man said.

Imran could hear their conversation clearly. The leather jacket man scratched his chin contemplatively for a few moments and then said, 'I am convinced that he is not wrong. It's there; our associates are just worthless. They lose their senses as soon as they hear the sounds.'

'But...what are those sounds anyway?'

'Whatever they may be. We shouldn't worry about them.'

'And how did both of them die?'

'That,' the jacket man said thoughtfully, 'I can't understand. Only he dies who begins the work. We have seen this from the beginning.'

'Then what should we do?' the other man said.

'We should wrap this issue up today,' the jacket man said. 'There is no police patrol there as well.'

'But there was someone in the house besides us

that night. My hunch is that it's the man who lives in that room outside the building.'

'Okay, get up. We shouldn't waste time.'

'Let's have a drink. I am very tired. What will you have? Whiskey or something else?'

Both of them started drinking. Imran got up and went to a phone booth nearby. A moment later he was dialling Fayyaz's private number.

'Hello, Super! Yes, it's me. Oh nothing; I have just caught a cold. I wanted to ask you if I should take some medicine for that? Aray, don't be angry. The other news is that there should be a police patrol around that building within the next one hour. That's it. Don't ask questions. If this doesn't happen, then next time Sherlock Holmes is not going to help Dr Watson.'

Returning to his seat, Imran sat down again. The leather jacketed man was saying to the other guy, 'The old man is not crazy. His calculations are never wrong.'

'Oonh. Whatever,' the other man said, slamming his glass on the table. 'Right or wrong, everything can go to hell. You tell me. What will you say if you happen to meet that girl again?'

'Oh!' the jacket man laughed. 'I will say—I am sorry, I don't recognize you.'

'Great! But what if she goes to the police?'

'She will never do such a thing. She will have to admit that she spent a night with me in that building; and besides, I don't think she will remember the key...'

After ordering coffee, Imran got busy with his second piece of chewing gum. He looked as if he was in his own world, but in reality he was digesting each and every word of the conversation.

'So will the old man come today?' the other man asked.

'Yes. Let's get it all sorted out today,' the man in the jacket said.

The two of them got up. Imran gulped down his coffee; he had already paid the bill. Both men got out of the restaurant and hailed a taxi. Soon, another taxi was in their pursuit. In the backseat of the second taxi, Imran was sitting with his legs pulled up, scratching his head. Sometimes, unknowingly, he acted mad even in private.

On reaching Murkeim Lane, the first taxi stopped. The two men got off and entered an alley. Here Imran was a bit careless. He saw them entering the alley, but by the time he paid the taxi, he had already lost them.

The alley was desolate. As he walked on, he saw another lane on his right. Crossing the second lane, he realized that there was a whole web of alleys there. He saw no point in wasting his time and came out on the main road again. He stopped at a bookstall some distance from the alley, looking at the colourful jackets of the books lined up. About five minutes later, a taxi stopped in front of the lane and a middle-aged man got off and paid the taxi. He had a brown beard, but Imran's attention was caught by his forehead. It looked familiar, and so did his eyes.

As soon as the man entered the alley, Imran did the same. After negotiating a few lanes, the old man stopped and knocked at a door. Imran was at some distance; because it was very dark, there was no risk of being seen. He jammed himself against a wall. The door opened and the old man entered, muttering something. The door closed again. It was a two storey building. Imran was left scratching his head, but he couldn't abandon this pursuit so easily. He reached the door, wondering how to get inside, and put his ear to the door. But the very next instant, the door was flung open and two men stood before him. He couldn't see their faces well because of the faint light coming from inside the building, but both of them seemed to be strongly built. 'Who is it?' one of them asked in a commanding voice.

'I am not late, am I?' Imran responded immediately.

There was no reply from the other side.

'Who are you?' the question was repeated from the other side.

'Three thirteen?' Imran replied like an idiot. Suddenly he was grabbed by his collar and pulled inside. Imran did not resist.

'Now tell me, who are you?' one of them said, pushing him.

'Take him inside,' the second one said.

They pushed him to a room where there were seven men sitting around a huge table along with the old man, the pursuit of whom had brought Imran here. He seemed to be the leader of this group because he was sitting at the head of the table.

All of them looked at Imran in surprise, but Imran, standing between the two men who had brought him there, was looking at the jacketed man.

'Aha!' Imran laughed abruptly and, rolling his eyes, he said to him, 'I will never forgive you. You have ruined my beloved's life!'

'Who are you? I don't know you,' the man said in astonishment.

'But I know you very well. You made romantic advances towards my beloved, I didn't say anything. You spent a night with her, I stayed quiet. But I cannot tolerate that now you have stopped meeting her altogether.'

'Why have you come here?' the old man snapped, staring at the two men who had brought in Imran. They told him the story. During this time, Imran went on staring at the jacket man. It seemed as if he had no interest in the rest of them. Then a punch landed on his jaw and he stumbled back a few steps. He bent down to pick up his felt hat and began dusting it as if it had dropped off his head accidentally. He was still staring at the jacketed man.

'Like a good and obedient rival lover in a romantic novel, I can disqualify myself in your favour,' Imran said to him.

'Shut your trap,' the old man shouted. 'I know you very well. Were you there that night?'

Imran did not bother to even look at him.

'Don't let him leave this place alive!' the old man said, jumping up.

'But only on one condition,' Imran smiled, 'that no one should be disrespectful to my dead body.'

There was not the slightest change in his foolish calmness. Two or three men came towards him. Immediately Imran snapped, 'Hands up!' and pulled out his hand from his pocket. The men paused, but the next moment they broke out into wild laughter. Instead of a revolver, Imran held a rubber doll in his hand. The old man's thunderous voice silenced them. They came for him again. When they were quite close, Imran pressed the doll's tummy. Its mouth opened and dark yellow smoke gushed out, spreading in a diameter of about three–four feet. The men started coughing and then fell unconscious.

'Don't let him escape!' the old man shouted again.

Imran then hit the electric lamp with something very heavy. The bulb exploded with a loud noise and the room fell into darkness. Imran covered his nose with a handkerchief and crept along the wall towards the corner of the table. There was quite a ruckus in the room. Perhaps all of them were practising punches on each other. Imran's hand slowly crawled over the corner of the table, but he was not unsuccessful. What he had been eyeing from the beginning was now in his hand: the old man's leather handbag.

On the way back to the door, someone tried to block his way. But he soon fell, lamenting his broken front teeth. Imran wanted to get out of the room as soon as possible because his throat was burning now. The smoke from the doll's mouth had now spread all over the room.

Leaving behind the noise of coughing and abuses, he reached the outside door. As soon as he exited the alley, he entered another one. It was dangerous to get out on the main road for now. For some time, he roamed around that intricate network of alleys and reached another main road. Some time later, he was sitting in a taxi, rubbing his lips as though he was removing lipstick marks after a tryst with a lover.

Chapter 10

NEXT MORNING BROUGHT ANOTHER headache for Captain Fayyaz. He had to get involved directly in the affair himself, otherwise the issue would have been handed to the civil police. The dead body of a young man had been discovered at about one or one and a half furlong from the haunted building. The dead man was wearing beige pants and a leather jacket. Following Imran's instructions, Captain Fayyaz had deputed a batch of police constables to guard the building. According to their report no one had come near the building, nor had there been any sound; but despite this, the body was found in the morning. When Captain Fayyaz heard this news he wondered why Imran had requested the police patrol around the building.

Upon reaching the spot, he examined the body. Someone had shot the man on the right temple. Constables told Fayyaz that they had not heard a gunshot either.

Perplexed at this incident, Captain Fayyaz set out for Imran's house. He was quite furious. He wondered what he would do if Imran, instead of telling him something useful, recited stupid verses of Mir and Ghalib. Sometimes he wanted to shoot him for his idiocies. But then what would become of Fayyaz's fame? All of his fame was because of Imran. Imran had solved many of his most complex problems for him. Imran did the work, and newspapers carried Fayyaz's name. This was the reason why Fayyaz had to put up with everything about Imran.

He found Imran at his home—but in strange circumstances: he was combing his servant Suleiman's hair; and advising him like a worried mother. As soon as Fayyaz entered the room, Imran punched Suleiman's back and said, 'Abay! Why didn't you tell me it was morning already!'

Suleiman ran off, laughing.

'Imran, when will you become a human?' Fayyaz said, falling on a sofa.

'I don't see any profit in becoming a human; however, I'd like to be an inspector.'

'As far as I am concerned you may like to go to hell but please tell me, why did you ask for the building to be guarded last night?'

'I don't remember,' Imran said dolefully. 'Did I really do such a thing?'

'Imran!' Fayyaz said angrily. 'Next time if I ask you for help, I'll be damned a thousand times over.'

'I think thousand is a bit low,' Imran said seriously. 'I am willing to consider if you increase it a bit.'

Fayyaz lost his patience. He thundered, 'Do you know that today we have found another body near that place about a furlong away?'

'Goodness!' Imran slapped his face.

Captain Fayyaz continued, 'I don't know why you want to keep me in the dark. If things get worse,

I will have to take care of them—but that will be very troublesome. Someone shot the man on his right temple. I don't understand who has done this...'

'Who could that be but Imran...?' Imran murmured and then asked seriously, 'Was there a patrol there?'

'There was.'

'Their report?'

'Absolutely nothing. They didn't even hear a gunshot.'

'I am not asking that. Did anyone try to enter the building yesterday as well?'

'No. But I was talking about the body.'

'Keep talking then. I won't stop you, but also keep answering my questions. What about the keeper of the grave? Is he still there or has he disappeared?'

'Imran, for God's sake, don't mess with me.'

'All right then. Ali Imran, MSc, PhD, doesn't wish to have a conversation.'

'Why are you after that madman?'

'Let it be. Now tell me something more about the body.'

'What else? I have already said everything. From his face, he doesn't appear to be a very old man. Young, handsome; was wearing a leather jacket and beige pants...'

'What?' Imran said with a start. He pursed his lips as though whistling and stared at Fayyaz. After a while, he heaved a sigh and said,

'Fearlessly Love leapt into Nimrod's fire
No difference was there between the slave and
the slave owner.'

'What nonsense!' Fayyaz said, annoyed. 'First of all, you don't even know the verses properly. And besides, this is no occasion for this. Imran, if I had the power, I'd shoot you.'

'Why, what was wrong with the couplet?'

'I have no interest in poetry, but I feel both the lines are disconnected. *La haula wala quwwat.* Even I get caught up in these lexical debates. For God's sake, let's talk about work.'

'I will talk about work tonight and you will be with me, but the patrol around that building should not be removed even for a second. Also, one of your men will have to stay in the room of the keeper of the grave. Now go away. I have already had my tea, otherwise I would have offered some to you too. Oh yes, please convey to my one-eyed beloved that the disgraced rival lover has been finished. Rest is all good.'

'Imran, I will not leave you alone so easily. You will have to tell me everything—here and now.'

'Okay, so listen: Lady Jehangir is about to become a widow. Will you try to get me married to her afterwards? Do you understand?'

'Imran!' Fayyaz was so angry that he could have hit him.

'Yes, boss.'

'Stop this nonsense! I will make your life difficult now.'

'And how will you do that, Super Fayyaz?'

'Very easily,' Fayyaz said, lighting his cigarette. 'Your family suspects that you spend your time loafing around and indulging in debaucheries, but they don't have concrete evidence. I will provide that evidence. It will not be difficult for me to arrange a woman who will come to your Amma bi and relate her tale of being dishonoured at your hands to her.'

'Oh!' Imran said, pursing his lips with a suspicious expression. He said, in a low voice, 'Amma bi's slippers are all-proof. Nonetheless, Super Fayyaz, you can try doing this as well. You will find me a patient and a thankful son. Here, have a chewing gum.'

'You will not have a place in this house,' Fayyaz said.

'Your house is there for me.'

'So you will not tell me?'

'Obviously not.'

'Okay, so now you will not interfere in these matters. I will look into these myself,' Fayyaz said coldly, getting up. 'And if you still interfere, then you will be in the grip of law.'

'Will this grip be on the legs or on my neck?' Imran asked seriously. He looked at Fayyaz for a few moments and then said, 'Wait.'

Fayyaz paused and looked at him helplessly.

Imran opened his cupboard and took out the leather bag he had filched from the unknown men last night. He opened the bag, took out a few papers, and handed them to Fayyaz. Fayyaz started as soon as he took a look at them. Soon he was racing through the rest of the papers.

'Where did you find these?' Fayyaz was almost out of breath. His hands trembled in excitement.

'In a junk shop. I found it with a great difficulty. Two annas a pound was the rate.'

'Imran! For the love of God!' said Fayyaz, still in a state of disbelief.

'What can poor Imran do?' Imran said with a dry expression. 'If he interferes, you will put him in the grip of law.'

'My dear Imran, please, for God's sake, be serious.'

'I am so serious you can feed me B.P. toffees.'

'Where did you find these papers?'

'On the road and I have conveyed them to the law. Now it is up to the law to find those hands that it can handcuff. Imran has stopped his interference.'

Fayyaz looked at him helplessly.

'But hear this,' Imran said, laughing loudly. 'Not even law's ghosts can reach those people.'

'All right. At least tell me how these papers are related to this,' Fayyaz said.

'You should know.' Imran immediately grew serious. 'I know only that these papers belong to the Foreign Office. But what could it mean if these thugs had them?'

'Which thugs?' Fayyaz said surprised.

'The same ones who were in the building...'

'My Lord!' Fayyaz muttered impatiently. 'But how did you get hold of these?'

Imran recounted the previous night's adventures to him. Fayyaz paced up and down the room impatiently. Sometimes he would pause and stare at Imran. When Imran had finished speaking, he said. 'Goodness! You did the wrong thing. Why didn't you inform me about this yesterday?'

'I am informing you now. I also gave you the address of the building. Do whatever you can,' he said.

'Should I go there to eat dust now?'

'What's wrong with that?'

'Do you know what kinds of papers are these?'

'They are pretty good. They can fetch a good sum as junk.'

'All right, I will leave,' Fayyaz said, gathering the papers and putting them in the bag.

'Will you take them like this?' Imran said. 'Don't. I might have to go look for your murderers.'

'Why?'

'Call and get a police escort to come over,' Imran said, laughing. 'They have been looking for me. I spent the night outside. Even now this house must be under surveillance. Anyway, tell me what these papers are all about.'

Fayyaz sat down again. He wiped the sweat on his forehead. After a pause, he said, 'These papers were stolen seven years ago. But these are not all of them. A responsible officer of the Foreign Office was travelling with them. I cannot tell you why and for what reason because that is a governmental secret. The officer was killed. His body was found, but travelling along with him was another man from the secret service. There has been no information regarding him till today. Possibly he was killed too, but his body was never found.'

'Aha! Then this is quite a big game!' Imran said, thinking. 'But I will try to put an end to it soon.'

'What will you do now?'

'It is too early to say anything,' Imran said. 'Listen now: keep these papers with you and leave the handbag with me. Actually take the handbag as well. I have a few ideas in my head. And yes...that building must be guarded at all times.'

'But why?'

'I will construct your shrine there,' Imran said, annoyed.

Fayyaz got up to call for the police escort.

558 206386 3207558

Chapter 11

THAT NIGHT IMRAN BARGED into Fayyaz's house completely flustered. Fayyaz was preparing to sleep and, if it had been someone other than Imran, he would been very rude. But things were different so far as Imran was concerned. Because of him, Fayyaz was able to get his hands on the papers that the Intelligence Bureau had been hunting for so long. Fayyaz asked him to come to his bedroom.

'I have come here to ask one thing only.'

'What is it, tell me?'

Imran said with a cold sigh, 'Will you visit my grave occasionally?'

Fayyaz wanted to slam Imran's head on the wall to give him a real excuse to visit a grave. But instead he just stared at him.

'Ah, you're silent,' Imran said like a betrayed lover. 'I get it! Perhaps you've fallen in love with someone else!'

'Imran, you son of a...'

'Son of Rahman,' Imran corrected him quickly.

'Why do you make my life miserable?'

'Oh, I see...Is your wife sleeping in another room?' Imran said, looking around.

'Stop this nonsense! Why have you come at this hour?'

'To show you a love letter,' Imran said, withdrawing a letter from his pocket. 'She does not have a husband, just a father.'

Fayyaz snatched the letter from his hand, wanting to tear it up.

'Unh huh...' Imran said, catching his hand. 'My dear, at least read it first. If you don't like it, its postage will be paid by the customer.'

Fayyaz took out the letter resentfully. But as soon as he started reading it, his vexation turned to amazement. The letter was typed.

Imran: If the leather handbag or its contents reach the police, then you'll be in trouble. It would be better if you return those, otherwise you will soon meet your death. Meet us near the Race Course tonight at eleven o'clock. Bring the handbag with you. Come alone. Otherwise, even if you bring along five thousand men, our bullet will find your chest.

After reading the letter Fayyaz looked at Imran.

'Give it back. I will return it,' Imran said.

'Are you mad?'

'Yes!'

'You are scared,' Fayyaz said.

'My heart nearly failed,' Imran said in a nasal voice.

'Do you have a revolver?'

'Revolver!' Imran said, putting his hands over his ears. 'Aray baap ray baap!'

'If you don't have one, I can get a licence for you.'

'No thanks. Have mercy on me,' Imran said, making a face. 'It emits smoke and also makes a noise. I have a weak heart. Come on. Give me the handbag.'

'What kind of childishness is this?'

'So you won't give it back?' Imran said, giving him a stern look.

'Stop talking nonsense. I am sleepy.'

'O you! Mister Fayyaz! I am still unmarried and I don't want to die without becoming a father.'

'The handbag has been sent to your father's office.'

'Then he will have to cry at the death of his son. Confucius said...'

'Please yaar, go now. Let me sleep.'

'It is fifty minutes to eleven,' Imran said, looking at the clock.

'All right, you can sleep here as well,' Fayyaz said helplessly.

After a few minutes, Imran said, 'Is there a patrol outside the building even now?'

'Yes. We have increased the number. But why are you doing all this? Officers keep asking me for reasons and I have to keep putting them off.'

'All right, get up then! Let's finish this game right now. We will get there in thirty minutes. We will have twenty minutes. Everything should be over by eleven, quarter past eleven.'

'What should be over?'

'I will tell you at half past eleven. Get up. In my head, I already see you rising in rank.'

'But why! What's so extraordinary?'

'Ali Imran, MSc, PhD, never utters anything that is ordinary, understand? Now get up!'

Fayyaz changed his clothes resentfully.

After a few minutes, his motorcycle was hurtling towards the village where the building was located. Upon reaching the building, Imran said to Fayyaz, 'The only thing you have to do is to keep the guardian of the grave engaged in conversation till I return. Understand? Go to his room. Don't leave him. Not even for a second.'

Chapter 12

ARMED GUARDS WERE POSTED around the building. The man in charge of the patrol recognized Fayyaz and saluted him. Fayyaz had a routine official exchange with him and then headed for the room of the guardian of the grave. The doors of the room were open, and inside the keeper seemed to be meditating. Hearing Fayyaz's footsteps, he opened his eyes. They were as red as smouldering coals.

'What is it?' he asked in a vexed tone.

'Nothing. I came to see if everything was all right,' Fayyaz said.

'I don't understand what is going on. Like those donkeys, even the police have gone mad.'

'Like who?'

'Those who think that there is a treasure buried under the grave of the martyr.'

'However it maybe,' Fayyaz said, 'we don't want to find dead bodies here every day. We will dig up the grave if we deem it necessary.'

'You will be burned!' the guardian thundered. 'You will spit blood...you will die!'

'Is there really a treasure in there?'

On hearing this, the keeper thundered even more violently. Fayyaz looked at his watch repeatedly. Imran had been gone for fifteen minutes now. Fayyaz kept the guardian involved in conversation. Suddenly they heard a strange cry. The guardian jumped and turned around. Behind him a large space could be seen in the wall. Fayyaz sprung up in astonishment. He had come into this room many times, but it had never occurred to him that there could be a secret door in this room. At once, the keeper let out a loud cry and ran into the opening. Fayyaz was utterly bewildered. He took out his torch and made his way through the doorway himself. He was surrounded by complete darkness. Perhaps he was walking in some kind of a basement. After walking for a while, he saw stairs. Here the silence was as deep as a cemetery. Fayyaz began to climb the stairs. When he reached the top, he found himself rising out of the grave of the martyr. The tombstone lay open like the lid of a box.

The circle of light made from Fayyaz's torch went around the room. Then Fayyaz saw the keeper of the grave on his way out from the room where the bodies had been found.

'You people have destroyed me!' he shouted when he saw Fayyaz. 'Come and see what you have done!' He entered the room again. Fayyaz quickly followed him.

The light from the torch fell on the wall where much of the plaster had worn off. Attached to the wall were three knives five inches apart from one another. Fayyaz stepped forward. Behind the worn-out plaster, there was a large compartment through which the sharp ends of the knives disappeared. There was nothing in the compartment except for these knives.

The keeper was looking at Fayyaz imperiously.

'What is all this?' Fayyaz asked the guardian, staring at him.

The grave keeper cleared his throat as if he wanted to say something. Then suddenly he rammed into Fayyaz's chest and bolted. Fayyaz fell on all fours. Before regaining balance, he had already taken out his revolver, but to no avail. The guardian had already jumped into the grave and disappeared.

Fayyaz got to his feet and ran in the direction of the grave, but he could find no trace of the keeper. He came out of the building. The constables on duty still held their positions and they knew nothing of any man running out of the building. No one had come out of the building.

Suddenly he thought of Imran. Where had he gone? Was he involved in this? What was there in that secret compartment? Everything had become clear. The secret of the dead bodies, three wounds five inches from each other. Suddenly someone put a hand on his shoulder. Fayyaz turned around with a start. Imran stood there making faces.

'So it was you,' Fayyaz said, looking at him from head to toe.

'Not was, I *am*! And I expect to live another three, four days.'

'What did you take out from there?'

'Are you hurt, my dear lover?' Imran said in a tearful voice. 'They cleaned it up before I got there. I wanted to examine the mechanism of the secret compartment, but the grave came apart as soon as I touched the lever.'

'But what was there?'

'The rest of the papers which were not in the leather handbag.'

'What! Oh idiot, why didn't you tell me before?' Fayyaz slapped his forehead. 'But how did they get inside the building?'

'Come, let me show you,' Imran said, taking him aside. He took Fayyaz to the western corner of the house. Here there were bushes about the height of a man growing alongside the wall. Imran pushed aside the bushes, turned on his torch, and Fayyaz's jaw dropped at what he saw. The wall had a hole large enough for a man to crawl through.

'This is terrible,' Fayyaz murmured.

'And where is that holy man?' asked Imran.

'He also escaped. But how did you get inside?'

'Through the same place. I thought of these bushes today...'

'What will you do now with the rest of the papers?' Fayyaz said helplessly.

'I'll return the rest of the papers. No point in just having half the papers. Whoever has the papers must possess all of them. After that, I will get this grave reserved in my name to spend the rest of my life here.'

Chapter 13

THE PHONE IN IMRAN'S room had been ringing for a long time. He was sitting nearby reading a book. He did not pay any attention, but when the ringing did not cease he slammed the book on the table and called out to his servant, Suleiman.

'Yes, sahib?' Suleiman asked as he entered the room.

'Go see which idiot is ringing the bell...'

'It's the phone, sahib.'

'Phone!' Imran said and glared at the phone. 'Pick it up and throw it out on the road.'

Suleiman picked up the receiver and presented it to Imran.

'Hello!' Imran shouted into the mouthpiece. 'Yes, yes. Who is it if not Imran? Do you hear a dog barking?'

'Why didn't you meet us near the Race Course last night?' said the voice at the other end.

'Get lost, you ass!' Imran addressed Suleiman without covering the mouthpiece.

'What did you say?' the voice roared.

'Oh...oh...I was saying this to Suleiman. He's my servant. Yes, so can you tell me why I didn't come to the Race Course last night?'

'I am asking you!'

'Then listen, my friend!' Imran said. 'I have not worked so hard for nothing. Someone has already offered ten thousand for the handbag. If you increase it a little, I am willing to make the deal with you.'

'You want trouble?'

'Yes, I met her. I like her very much.' Imran winked.

'We will wait for you tonight. After this, your body will be found in some sewer of the city tomorrow.'

'Oh, thanks for letting me know in advance. Now I won't leave the house without my coffin.'

'I am making it clear again...'

'Understood,' Imran said in an obedient voice and hung up. He picked up his book from where he left and busied himself as though nothing had happened.

A little later, the phone rang again. Imran picked up the receiver and said in an annoyed voice, 'Now I will give away this phone to some orphanage, understand? I am a very dizzy man... Did I just say dizzy? No, not dizzy, busy. I am a busy man.'

'You mentioned an offer right now?' the voice at the other end said.

'Not a coffer, a fountain pen!' Imran said.

'Don't waste time,' the voice said in an annoyed tone. 'We are also willing to offer ten thousand for it.'

'Very good!' Imran said. 'Then it is decided. You will get the bag.'

'Tonight.'

'Do you know me well?' Imran asked.

'As well as an index finger knows the middle finger.'

'Good.' Imran snapped his finger. 'Then you must already know that I am an eternal fool.'

'You...'

'Yes, I. Race Course is a very desolate place. If you shoot me after taking the bag, who will I go to?'

'This will not happen,' the voice said.

'I say you send one of your men with the money to Tip Top Nightclub. I swear by Madhubala's youth that I will return the bag.'

'If there is some mischief then...'

'Punish me by making me stand like a hen...'[1]

'Okay. Remember you will be within a revolver's range.'

'Don't worry. I have never even seen a revolver.' Imran replaced the handset and started searching his pocket for his packet of chewing gum.

---

[1] *Murgha banana*: 'to assume the position of a cock' is a form of corporal punishment, in which a child bends his head down to his knees and with his hands around his knees pulls his own ears.

Chapter 14

WITH THE LEATHER HANDBAG pressed tightly under his arm, Imran reached Tip Top Nightclub exactly at eight. Almost all the tables had been taken. Imran examined the crowd standing near the bar. His eyes paused at a table where Lady Jehangir was sitting with a young lady, drinking white wine. Imran walked up to her slowly.

'My lady!' he said and bowed respectfully.

Lady Jehangir raised her right brow and gave him a sharp glance, and then began to smile.

'Hel...lo...Imran...!' she said, raising her right hand. 'It's always pleasant to spend time with you. This is Miss Tasneem. Khan Bahadur Zafar Tasneem's daughter. And this is Ali Imran...'

'MSc, PhD,' Imran interjected foolishly.

'Very pleased to meet you!' said Tasneem. Her accent seemed to mimic Imran's.

'I feel displeased.'

'Why?' Lady Jehangir asked in an astonished voice.

'I thought her name was Gulfam.'

'What nonsense is this!' Lady Jehangir was rankled.

'I am telling you the truth! It seemed like it to

me. I don't think Tasneem suits her. It sounds like a name for someone who is infected with tuberculosis. Someone whose back is bent like the name.'

'I think you are drunk.' Lady Jehangir tried to change the subject. 'Here, drink some more.'

'Is this faluda?' Imran asked.

'My dear Tasneem,' Lady Jehangir said quickly. 'Please don't mind what he's saying. He is a humorous one. And Imran, please have a seat.'

'What is there to mind anyway?' Imran said, exhaling a sigh. 'I will remember her as Gulfam.'

Tasneem was feeling extremely embarrassed and also a little sorry about trying to make fun of him.

'I will leave now,' Tasneem said, standing up.

'So will I,' Imran said, getting up.

'My dears! Both of you please sit,' Lady Jehangir said, holding both of them by their hands.

'No, I just remembered that I had an important thing to do,' Tasneem said, and left after gently having released her hand from Lady Jehangir's grip.

'And I,' Imran said, placing his hand on his chest, 'can sacrifice everything for you.'

'Shut up! Liar...You upset me for no reason.'

'I worship you, sweetheart, but while your old, decrepit husband is alive...'

'You are making fun of him again?'

'No, dearest, if I am your moon, then you're my moonlight. If your heart doesn't...'

'That's enough. You act like such a rascal sometimes.'

'I am sorry,' said Imran. As he said this, his eyes paused at a table near them. A familiar looking man was staring at him. Imran picked up the handbag from the table and pressed it under his armpit. Suddenly the man winked at him and smiled. In response, Imran winked with both his eyes, one by one. Lady Jehangir was looking at her glass. Perhaps in her mind was brewing some deeply romantic idea.

'I will be back,' Imran said to Lady Jehangir and left for the man's table.

'Did you bring it?' the man whispered.

'What is this then?' Imran pointed to the handbag. 'Did you bring it?'

'Yes, yes!' the man said, placing his hand on the handbag he had brought.

'That's good then,' Imran said. 'Hold this and quietly slip out of here.'

'Why?' he glared.

'Captain Fayyaz suspects me. It is quite possible that he has appointed some men to watch over me.'

'This is not some trick, is it?'

'Not at all. I am in dire need of money these days.'

'If you try to play a trick, you will not live,' the man said, taking the handbag and standing up.

'My friend, I am not taking this money to build my own mausoleum,' Imran said in a low voice as he watched the man walk out. Imran had a mischievous smile on his face. He grabbed the bag the man had given him and returned to sit close to Lady Jehangir again.

Chapter 15

As soon as the man left the building, two men lurking in the compound of the nightclub approached him.

'What happened?' the first one asked.

'I got it,' the one with the bag said.

'Does it have the papers?'

'I didn't open to see it.'

'Idiot.'

'How could I have opened it there?'

'Bring it here,' the first one said, taking the bag from him. Then he said in a surprised voice, 'Why is this so heavy?' He tried to open it, but there was a lock on the bag.

'Come on, let's get out of here,' the third one said. 'No need to open it here.'

They came out of the compound and got into a car and drove away. Once they were out of the populated areas they switched on the car's interior lights. One of the men, who seemed to be the oldest but also the strongest of them all, tried to open the bag using a thin wire. As soon as the flap of the handbag was lifted, the two men sitting in the rear seat jumped. Something sprung out of the bag and hit the driver's head, almost making the car crash into a tree. There were three big frogs bouncing around in the car. The old man swore and one guy started laughing.

'Shut up!' the old man bellowed from deep within his throat. 'You're an idiot! It is because of you...'

'Sir, what could I have done! How could I have opened it there? Even he thought there could be police there.'

'Cut out this nonsense! I had already checked. There was no police there. Don't take me for an ordinary guy. Now this lad has invited his death. Hey you! Stop the car.'

The car stopped. The old man thought quietly for a while and then said, 'Who else was there in the club with him?'

'A good-looking woman. Both of them were drinking.'

'Wrong! Imran doesn't drink.'

'But he was drinking, sir!'

The old man began to think again.

'Come on! Let's go back.' After a few moments of silence, he said, 'I will kill him in the club.'

The car turned towards the city again.

'I think he might already be dead,' the man sitting next to the old man said.

'No. He's not an idiot like you,' the old man said angrily. 'If he has deceived us, he is certainly aware of it.'

'Then he must have left the club...'

'Don't argue with me,' the old man thundered. 'I will hunt him down and kill him. Even if he's in his own house.'

Chapter 16

IMRAN SAT AT HIS table for a few moments and then suddenly darted out of the club. He heard a car start in the compound. He came back in.

'Why are you running around?' Lady Jehangir asked, her eyes hazy with drink.

'Trying to digest the food,' Imran said, looking at his wristwatch. Lady Jehangir laughed with her mouth closed. Imran's eyes were still on his watch. After a while, he got up again. Now he was heading towards the telephone booth. He picked up the receiver, dialled a number, and began to talk.

'Hello, Super Fayyaz...This is Imran...Leave immediately.'

Replacing the receiver, he returned to the club hall but did not sit near Lady Jehangir this time. For a few moments, he stood and looked around. Then he went and sat at a table with three men. These men knew Imran, so they did not mind him joining them.

For about fifteen minutes, Imran laughed and joked with them, but during this period his eyes would repeatedly return to the door.

Suddenly he spotted, at the door the old man from whom he had snatched the handbag a few days ago. Imran's conversation grew even more animated but he soon felt something prodding his right shoulder. From the corner of his eye he looked towards his right and saw that the old man was standing right next to them. His left hand was in his coat pocket and a hard object from the coat pocket was poking Imran's shoulder. Imran knew that this could only be the barrel of a revolver.

'Imran sahib!' the old man said very politely. 'Will you please step out for a few minutes?'

'Aha! Uncle dear!' Imran chuckled. 'Most certainly! But I have some complaints about you, and therefore you shouldn't have any complaints about me as well.'

'For sure. Please step out,' the old man smiled. 'I am sorry for that idiot's actions.'

Imran stood up. Now he could feel the barrel of the revolver digging into his side. The two of them came out. As soon as they reached the park outside, both the old man's companions joined them.

'Where are the papers?' the old man asked, grabbing Imran's collar and shaking him. There was complete silence in the park. Suddenly Imran caught the old man's left hand and landed a powerful punch under his chin. Now the revolver was in Imran's hand. The old man stumbled and was about to fall to the ground when he was helped by his men.

'I ask you: where is that ten thousand?' Imran yelled.

Suddenly, from behind the balsam fence nearby, some eight or ten men pounced on the three men and a violent battle ensued. The three men fought with remarkable courage and audacity.

'Super Fayyaz!' Imran shouted. 'The man with the beard...!'

The bearded man was making a break for it. He was about to clear the balsam fence when a spark flew from Imran's revolver. The bullet hit the man on his leg.

'Aray baap! Aray baap!' Imran cried out as he threw the gun down and started slapping his face.

The other two men had been nabbed by this time. Fayyaz leapt towards the old man who was still struggling to escape. Fayyaz caught him by his leg and dragged him out of the fence.

'Who is he?' Fayyaz shone a light on his face. A crowd had gathered in the park upon hearing the gunshot.

The old man was not unconscious. He was writhing like a wounded snake. Imran bent and pulled off his fake beard.

'Hain!' Fayyaz cried out. 'Sir Jehangir!'

Jehangir tried to run again, but Imran's kick kept him from doing so.

'Yes, Sir Jehangir,' Imran muttered. 'A foreign spy. A traitor to his nation.'

Chapter 17

THE FOLLOWING DAY, CAPTAIN Fayyaz sat in Imran's room staring at him incredulously as he talked. 'I am happy that because of me, a major spy and traitor has been brought to justice. Who could have imagined that a highly respected and venerable person like Sir Jehangir could be a spy for a foreign country?'

'But who was the guardian of the grave?' Fayyaz asked impatiently.

'Don't interrupt me while I speak. That poor man was trying to cross this hurdle by himself, but I spoilt his game. Last night I met him. He recounted the whole story. Perhaps he has now disappeared forever. He has been defeated in a major way. Now he doesn't want to show his face to anyone.'

'But who is he anyway?'

'Ayaz! Don't be surprised. I'll explain. This Ayaz was the same guy who was travelling with the Foreign Office secretary. He had half the papers and the secretary had the other half. When they were robbed, the secretary was killed and Ayaz somehow survived. The criminals could only get half the papers. Ayaz worked for the secret service of the Foreign Office. He survived but never reported to his office. Actually he was a highly prized officer in his time. This defeat convinced him that he shouldn't present himself in the office without retrieving the rest of the papers. He also knew half of the papers were of no use to anyone. The criminals would look for him to get the rest of the papers. In a few days, he uncovered the criminals but could not trace their chief. Days passed but Ayaz had no luck.

Then one day he set a new trap. He bought that building and started living there with his faithful servant. During this time, to implement his scheme he "discovered" a grave and laid out all that mechanism. Suddenly his servant fell ill and died. Ayaz devised another stratagem. He buried his servant and, after disguising himself, adopted his servant's life. Before this, he had legally transferred the building to Judge sahib and allotted one room for himself. Immediately after this, he started luring the criminals towards the building. He used ploys to make the criminals believe that the man who died was actually the secret service person and that the rest of the papers were hidden somewhere in the building. Recently, they secured access to the room where the dead bodies were found. The papers were actually in that secret wall compartment. They obtained clues regarding that from Ayaz again. As soon as someone came close to the wall with the secret compartment, Ayaz would make terrifying noises from beneath the tombstone. Whoever was near the wall would lean against it out of fear. Then Ayaz would bring the mechanism into action and the three blades would pierce the man's back. He did all this just to capture the chief, but the chief fell into my hands instead. Now Ayaz will never reveal himself. And dear Captain Fayyaz—I have promised him that his name will not appear anywhere in the case. Understand? And you will have to keep the promise I have made. Write your report in a way that even my one-eyed beloved is not mentioned either.'

'That's fine,' Fayyaz said quickly. 'Where are those ten thousand rupees you received from Sir Jehangir?'

'Yes.' Imran rolled his eyes. 'Let's go halves with it.'

'Nonsense! I will put the money in official custody,' Fayyaz said.

'Never!' Imran snapped up the leather handbag that he had got the previous night from one of Sir Jehangir's men.

Fayyaz snatched the handbag from him and began to open it.

'Beware! Be cautious....' Imran shouted like a chowkidar, but Fayyaz had already opened the bag. He cried out, 'Aray baap ray!' and sprang onto the sofa. A snake emerged out of the handbag and started crawling on the floor.

'May God wreck you! Imran—you rascal!' Fayyaz roared, standing on the sofa. The snake raised its hood and made a dash for the sofa. Fayyaz shouted fearfully and jumped onto another chair. The chair toppled and Fayyaz fell on his face. If Imran had not swiftly stepped on the snake's head, it would have certainly bitten Fayyaz. The rest of the snake's body coiled powerfully around Imran's shin, making him feel as though it would break. On top of this, Fayyaz was raining punches and slaps on him. With great difficulty he rid himself of both of them.

'You have lost it completely...you lunatic...savage...' Fayyaz yelled.

'What can I do, darling? Anyway, now you can hand this into official custody. If I had miscalculated last night, this thing would have put me in God's custody forever.'

'You mean Sir Jehangir...?'

'Yes. Last night we exchanged frogs and snakes!' Imran said and started chewing his gum in a glum manner. And then his face took on that foolish expression again.

SHOOTOUT AT THE ROCKS

Chapter 1

COLONEL ZARGHAM WAS RESTLESSLY pacing up and down his room.

He was a middle-aged man with an imposing, dignified face, and his bushy moustache tilted downward on his face. He shrugged his shoulders every few seconds as if his coat was slipping off his shoulders. This was an old habit: he compulsively twitched his shoulders at least once every two minutes. He glanced at the wall clock apprehensively and then went to stand near the window.

In the distance, the third week's moon was emerging from behind the mountains. The weather was pleasant and the view from the window delightful. But neither of those could put Colonel Zargham at ease.

Suddenly he heard footsteps approaching. He turned around with a start: at the door stood his beautiful young daughter, Sophiya.

'Oh Daddy, it's ten already but...'

'Yes, yes,' Zargham said reflectively. 'I think the train's late.'

He started looking out of the window again. Sophiya stepped towards him and placed her hand on his shoulder, but he went on looking outside.

'Why are you so disturbed?'

'Uff!' the colonel said, turning around. 'Don't these events matter to you?'

'I've never said that,' Sophiya said. 'I only meant to say, what's the point in worrying by overanalysing things?'

'What can I do? My trouble increases every passing moment.'

'Any new development?' There was an element of surprise in Sophiya's expression.

'Haven't you seen Captain Fayyaz's telegram?'

'I have seen it and that's what I have come to speak to you about.'

'Hmm. So has it troubled you as well?'

'Yes! What does he mean? He has written that he's sending someone who could be of great use to us if we don't get fed up with him. I say why send a man who will cause us trouble in the first place. And besides, he's not an official person anyway.'

'Yes, this disturbs me as well,' said the colonel, looking at the clock again. 'After all, what kind of a person is he sending and why would we get fed up with him?'

'Why didn't he send someone from his own department?' Sophiya objected.

'He could have if he wanted to, but Fayyaz is a principled man. For a private matter, he did not consider it appropriate to send someone official.'

Chapter 2

COLONEL ZARGHAM'S NEPHEWS, ANWAR and Arif, were at the station waiting for the train's arrival. They were there to receive someone sent by the Intelligence Bureau's Superintendent, Captain Fayyaz, upon their uncle's request. The train was an hour late.

These two brothers were good-looking, intelligent and well educated. Anwar was just two years older than Arif. For this reason, they were like friends, and Arif called Anwar by his first name. Both of them had also seen Captain Fayyaz's telegram and were curious.

'Captain Fayyaz's telegram was so strange,' Arif said.

'This damn train had to be late today,' Anwar muttered.

'But what kind of a person would he be?' Arif said.

'Whatever. I imagine him to be an irascible, grumpy fellow,' said Anwar. 'Colonel sahib is a bored man, and he bores others as well.'

'You are being unfair,' said Arif. 'In these circumstances you would have done the same.'

'Oh, forget it. What circumstances, which circumstances? It's just his superstitions. I often wonder how such a superstitious officer was given the command of a full battalion. It just doesn't make any sense: when cats purr in his backyard, he takes it to mean that some trouble will befall his family; he's scared out of his wits if he hears an owl hooting; if someone keeps a fork and knife crossed, it is a bad omen; if he sees a person blind in one eye first thing in the morning, it means danger...'

'But in this matter, I sympathize with him...' Arif said.

'But I feel angry,' Anwar said, irritated.

'One must forgive old men.'

'Old man?' Anwar said annoyed. 'I don't see anything old in him, except for his antique beliefs.'

'In any case, he's a legacy of the bygone era.'

They were interrupted by a sharp whistle—the train was arriving. This was a small hill station. Here, a whistle was blown to alert the passengers. There were eight or ten men on the platform. Among them were the haughty coolies in blue uniforms who strutted as if they were more important than even the station master; the food hawker who now lifted his lantern in a mesh-container from the bench onto his shoulders; and the pan-beedi seller, loudly singing a vulgar song, who too lifted his tray and hung it around his neck.

The train slowly crawled to the platform.

Three men disembarked from the train: two old countrymen and a young man wearing a khaki gabardine suit. A gun wrapped in a cover hung from his left shoulder. In his right hand, he held a large suitcase.

He was probably the one for whom Anwar and Arif were waiting.

'Has Captain Fayyaz sent you?' Anwar asked him.

'He couldn't have, if I didn't want to come myself,' the passenger replied, smiling.

'Of course! That's right, that's right!' Anwar added quickly.

'What's right?' the passenger asked, blinking his eyes.

Anwar was caught off guard. 'This...All this that you just said.'

'Oh, okay!' the passenger remarked as though he had understood differently.

Arif and Anwar exchanged meaningful glances.

'We have come to pick you up,' Arif said.

'Then please pick me up,' the passenger said, dropping his suitcase on the platform and sitting upon it.

Anwar called out to the coolie.

'What?' the passenger asked in an astonished tone. 'Would this one coolie be able to pick me up along with the suitcase?'

'Not at all,' Anwar said in a mischievous tone. 'Please stand up.'

The passenger stood up. Anwar gestured to the coolie to lift the luggage and grabbed the passenger's hand, 'Walk like this.'

'*La haula wala quwwat!*' Imran shook his head. 'I thought it would be something else.'

Anwar turned to Arif, 'I guess by now you must've understood the telegram.'

Arif laughed as the passenger walked past them with a serious expression on his face. They came out of the station and got into the car. Anwar sat in the backseat with the passenger, while Arif drove the car.

Anwar turned to Arif. 'Colonel sahib and Captain Fayyaz seem to have a humorous side to their relationship.' Arif laughed loudly. Both of them were thinking they would have a good time with this dumb-looking passenger.

Suddenly Anwar addressed the passenger, 'What's your good name, please?'

'Very good,' the passenger replied seriously.

Both of them laughed.

'Hain? What is so funny here?' the passenger asked.

'I asked your name,' Anwar said.

'Ali Imran, MSc, PhD.'

'MSc *and* PhD as well?' Arif laughed.

'Why did you laugh?' Imran asked.

'Oh—I laughed at something else,' Arif quickly clarified.

'All right, now you should permit me to laugh too,' Imran said and started laughing like a fool, making the other two laugh even more. Imran laughed louder still. After a while, Anwar and Arif both felt as if they themselves had been made fools of.

The car drove upward along the winding, mountainous roads. Everyone became quiet. Imran did not ask them their names.

Anwar was anticipating some amusement ahead. Colonel sahib's annoyance would be a spectacle worth watching! This fool would shut him up; someone like Imran would certainly drive him mad!

Anwar was right. Colonel Zargham was a man of disagreeable humour. He often lost his temper if he had to repeat himself twice.

In about half an hour, the car reached its destination. The colonel was still pacing restively in the same room and Sophiya was with him. Zargham scanned Imran from head to toe with a derisive look, and then smiled, 'Captain Fayyaz is good?'

'Oh, please! He's a rank imbecile,' Imran said, seating himself on the sofa. He took off the gun from his shoulder and put it against the arm of the sofa.

'Why? Why an imbecile?' the colonel asked in an astonished voice.

'For no special reason,' Imran said seriously. 'I think there is no reason for imbecility.'

'Very good!' Zargham stared at him. 'And your good person?'

'Oh. Hehe,' Imran giggled. 'I don't think it is appropriate to talk about my own goodness myself,' Imran said coyly.

Anwar could not suppress his laughter. As soon as he cracked up, Arif also started laughing.

'What is this incivility!' The colonel turned to them.

Both of them immediately fell silent and looked away to conceal their embarrassment. Sophiya was looking at Imran with a strange expression on her face.

'I asked your name,' the colonel said to Imran as he cleared his throat.

'When?' Imran said with a start.

'Just now!' the colonel replied explosively and the two brothers broke into laughter. They left the room stuffing their mouths with handkerchiefs.

'These lads are in trouble!' Zargham said angrily, and left the room quickly. It looked like he was going to run after them.

Imran sat there like a fool as if he had not seen or heard anything. Sophiya was alone in the room with him and there was a mischievous twinkle in her eye.

'You didn't tell us your name?' Sophiya said.

Upon this, Imran repeated his name along with his academic degrees. Sophiya had a look of disbelief on her face.

'Do you know the reason for being summoned here?' she asked.

'Reason!' Imran said with a start. 'Yes, of course! I know the reason. This is precisely why I've brought my air gun with me.'

'Air gun!' Sophiya said with astonishment.

'Yes,' Imran said seriously. 'I don't kill flies with my hands.'

The colonel, who was standing at the door, had overheard this conversation. He stepped forward, completely provoked now.

'I don't understand why Fayyaz has committed this idiocy!' he said grimly and glared at Imran.

'See, he's an imbecile. I told you so,' Imran chuckled.

'You should return by the first train in the morning,' Zargham said.

'No,' Imran said sternly. 'I have come with a weeklong plan.'

'No. Thank you very much,' the colonel said in vexed tone. 'I am ready to let you go with half your pay. How much would that be, anyway?'

'That depends on the number of flies,' Imran said, shaking his head. 'Generally speaking, I kill about a dozen and a half in an hour, and...'

'Enough!' the colonel said, lifting up his hand. 'I don't have time for nonsense.'

'Daddy, please...' Sophiya interjected. 'Don't you remember the subject of the telegram?'

'Hunh.' Zargham was thoughtful. His eyes were fixed on Imran who sat foolishly blinking his eyes.

'You are right,' the colonel said. And now his eyes shifted from Imran to his gun. He stepped forward and lifted the gun. As soon as he took out the gun from the cover, he had a fit. 'What nonsense!' he bellowed. 'This is *really* an air gun!'

There was absolutely no change in Imran's composure. He shook his head. 'I never lie.'

Colonel Zargham was so enraged that his daughter had to take him out of the room. The colonel did not care about anyone except Sophiya. Anyone else trying to do the same would have been strangled to death. Imran merely smiled, as if it had been a very pleasant encounter.

Sophiya returned some time later and showed Imran to his room without saying a word to him.

Chapter 3

THE CLOCK STRUCK ONE and Imran got out of bed. He opened the door and came out of the room. Silence reigned everywhere, but not a single light had been turned off in any of the rooms in the bungalow.

He stepped out into the verandah and waited to hear any footsteps or sounds, and then he darted into the room where the colonel's family was assembled. Except for Sophiya, everyone had a rifle next to themselves. Anwar and Arif looked extremely bored, Sophiya's eyes were bloodshot due to lack of sleep, and the colonel was sitting on the sofa, still as a statue. He was not even blinking his eyes. Upon seeing Imran, he twitched.

'What is it? Why have you come here?' he thundered.

'Something is bothering me,' Imran replied.

'What?' said the colonel. His demeanour did not soften.

'If you are troubled by a few unknown men, why don't you inform the police?'

'I know that the police cannot do anything.'

'Are those people really unknown to you?'

'Yes.'

'It doesn't make sense.'

'Why?'

'It's pretty straightforward. If you don't know them, why are you afraid of them?'

Instead of giving him a reply, the colonel went on staring at Imran.

'Sit down,' he said after a few moments. Imran took a seat.

'I know them,' the colonel said.

'Then the police should be contacted. Isn't it obvious?'

'Do you take me for a fool?' Zargham said in a displeased tone.

'Yes, of course!' Imran said, nodding his head seriously.

'What!' The colonel sprang up.

'Please sit down,' Imran said, lifting his hand distractedly. 'I say this because all of you could become the target of their bullets any time.'

'How?'

'They can enter the building any time they please.'

'No, they can't. There are guards patrolling out there...'

'Then what is the meaning of these rifles placed in front of you!' Imran shook his head. 'No, Colonel sahib! If you want to get work out of Ali Imran, MSc, PhD, you will have to apprise him of all the circumstances. I have not come here to be your bodyguard.'

'Daddy, please tell him...It is all right...' Sophiya said.

'Do you consider this man trustworthy?'

'She's just a child.' Imran pointed to Sophiya. 'Even

old, decrepit women trust me with everything.'

Sophiya was taken aback and stared blankly at Imran. She didn't know how to react. Anwar and Arif began to laugh.

'Shut your mouths!' the colonel yelled. Both of them made a face and became quiet.

'Tell me about those men,' Imran said.

Zargham was silent for a while and then said, 'I don't know what should I tell you.'

'Have you seen any of them during all this time?'

'No.'

'Then I guess I have gone mad!' Imran said.

The colonel stared at him. He was quiet for a while and then said, 'I recognize the mark of these people. I have found it in my house. It means I am in danger.'

'Ooh!' Imran pursed his lips as though he was whistling, then asked in a low voice, 'When did you find it?'

'Four days ago.'

'Good! Can I see it?'

'I don't think you can handle this business,' the colonel said in a tired voice. 'You must return tomorrow.'

'It is quite possible I can become a handler and a businessman. Please show it to me.'

Colonel Zargham was quiet for a while. He made a face to show his displeasure and got up to open a drawer. Imran observed him with interest. The colonel pulled out something from the drawer and returned to the sofa. Imran extended his hand. Anwar and Arif exchanged glances as if they expected some foolishness from Imran.

The colonel placed an object on the small round table. It was a three-inch long wooden monkey. Imran picked it up from the table. He examined it for a while, then replaced it and looked at the colonel.

'Can I ask you something?' Imran said.

'Just ask me. Don't bore me.'

'Wait!' Imran lifted his hand. Then he glanced at Sophiya and the others and said, 'It is quite possible you wouldn't want to answer my questions in their presence.'

'Oh, come on! Don't bore me,' the colonel said wearily.

'As you please. I only meant it as a warning,' Imran said carelessly. Then he stared at the colonel and said, 'Have you been associated with the illegal drug trade as well?'

The colonel sprang from his seat and looked at Imran as if he had just been stung. Then he quickly turned towards the boys, 'You go and sleep.'

The nephews' faces lit up but Sophiya didn't want to leave.

'You should go as well,' the colonel said with an agitated movement of his hand.

'Is it necessary?' Sophiya said.

'Go away, now!' Zargham colonel shouted and all three of them left the room.

'Yes, what did you say?' The colonel turned towards Imran.

131

Imran repeated his question.

'So you know something about this?' the colonel pointed to the wooden monkey.

'A lot,' Imran said nonchalantly.

'How do you know?'

'It is very hard to explain.' Imran smiled. 'But you have still not answered my question.'

'No, I have never been associated with the drug trade.'

'Then,' Imran said thoughtfully, 'you know something about them. Why else did this object enter this building?'

'By God!' Zargham said as he rubbed his hands nervously. 'You seem to be a very useful man.'

'But I am returning tomorrow morning.'

'Absolutely not! Absolutely not!'

'If I don't return tomorrow, then who will watch over that hen which I left sitting over the eggs?'

'Good lad. This is not the time to make fun.'

'You are afraid of Li Yu Ka?' Imran said, shaking his head.

Once again the colonel jumped, this time as if Imran had stung him.

'Who *are* you!' the colonel said in a terrified voice.

'Ali Imran, MSc, PhD.'

'And have you *really* been sent here by Captain Fayyaz?'

'And I am returning tomorrow morning.'

'Impossible, impossible! I cannot let you go at any cost. But how do you know about Li Yu Ka?'

'I cannot tell you,' Imran said. 'But I can tell you

a lot about Li Yu Ka himself. He is the key. There is a lot of illegal drug trade in his name but no one has ever seen him.'

'Absolutely right. My boy, you look dangerous to me.'

'I am the biggest dunce in the world.'

'Nonsense! But how do you know all this?' Zargham muttered. 'What if you are one of his men?' he said fearfully, his voice sticking in his throat.

'Good. Tomorrow morning I will...'

'No, no!' the colonel shouted, protesting with his hands.

'Then tell me, how did this wooden monkey reach you?' Imran asked.

'I don't know,' the colonel said.

'I think you are trying to test this fool's foolishness,' Imran said seriously. 'All right, then listen: Li Yu Ka is a two hundred year old name...'

'Dear lad! Where did you get this information?' the colonel said, looking at him admiringly. 'No one has this information except Li Yu Ka's gang.'

'Then should I assume that you have been a part of Li Yu Ka's gang?' Imran said.

'Absolutely not! You have misunderstood me...'

'Then how did this insignia reach you? What do those people demand of you?'

'Oh! You know this too!' Zargham cried out. He began pacing about the room again. There was a mischievous smile on Imran's lips.

'Lad!' The colonel abruptly stopped in his tracks. 'You will have to prove that you are the same person who was sent by Captain Fayyaz.'

'You look very upset,' Imran laughed. 'I have Fayyaz's letter with me. But why are you so upset? This is just the first warning. After the monkey, they will send you a snake. If you still don't meet their demand, then they will send a rooster—and then you will be wiped off the next day. But what is their demand in the first place?'

The colonel fell silent. His jaw had dropped and his eyes were glued to Imran's face. 'But,' he said, moistening his lips with his tongue, 'how are you still alive, knowing all this?'

'Simply because of Coca Cola.'

'Serious! Be serious!' The colonel said, lifting his hand. 'Show me Fayyaz's letter.'

Imran handed him Fayyaz's letter. Zargham looked at the letter for a while, then returning the letter to Imran, he said, 'I don't understand what kind of a man you are!'

'Of all kinds. For now, don't think about me,' said Imran. 'The sooner you tell me about your situation, the better it will be for you.'

The colonel's face showed signs of reluctance. He didn't speak.

'Okay, wait,' Imran said after a little while. 'Li Yu Ka's men do such things only on one condition. It is a gang that illegally trades in drugs. No one knows who Li Yu Ka is, but all the profits from the trade are funnelled to him. Sometimes, some of his agents betray him and they don't meet his demands. Only in these conditions, the agents get such warnings: first threat, the monkey; second threat, the snake; and the third one, the rooster. If they don't meet the demands by the third threat, they are killed.'

'So you think I am Li Yu Ka's agent?' The colonel cleared his throat.

'What else can I think in such circumstances?'

'No, that is incorrect.'

'Then?'

'I think I have some...information about Li Yu Ka's whereabouts,' the colonel muttered.

'Clues to whereabouts! How come?'

'Some papers which can put Li Yu Ka in danger.'

'Putting him in danger is different. But clues to his whereabouts!' Imran shook his head in dissent.

'This is my opinion...'

'But how did you arrive at this conclusion?'

'It is hard to explain. However, I could not understand the papers at all.'

'But how did you get those?'

'Quite amazingly, actually!' Colonel Zargham said, lighting his cigar. 'I was in Hong Kong during the last World War. That's where I got my hands on those papers. And the reality is that the person who handed me the papers mistook me for someone else. It happened like this: one night I was sitting in a hotel in Hong Kong when a slender Chinese man came and sat down at my table. I sensed he was very scared. His whole body was trembling. He produced a large envelope from his pocket, placed it on my lap from under the table and spoke quietly, 'I am in danger, get these to B-14.' And before I could say anything, he swiftly ran out of the hotel. It was an astonishing thing, so I quietly kept the envelope in my pocket. I thought he must be someone from the Chinese military service who wanted me to convey some important papers to some section called 'B-14'.

'At that time I was in full uniform. I returned to my lodging and removed the envelope from my pocket. It was sealed. I left it as it is. The following day I made some inquiries about B-14, but there was no such thing in the military secret service. There was, in fact, no trace of any B-14, in all of Hong Kong. Frustrated, I finally opened the envelope.'

'So was there a report regarding Li Yu Ka in there?' Imran asked.

'No. They were some trade-related papers. But it was clear what the nature of the trade was. There was a recurrent mention of Li Yu Ka in them. Many of those papers are in Chinese and Japanese, which I was unable to understand.'

'Then how did you find out about Li Yu Ka's history?'

'Oh, that. I did some background research regarding Li Yu Ka in Hong Kong. I discovered everything except Li Yu Ka's identity and his whereabouts. His agents are apprehended regularly, but no one has ever been able to locate him. Besides, this name has been around for about two hundred years now.'

Imran was quiet for a while and then asked, 'So how long have these people been after you?'

'It's not something recent,' the colonel said, lighting up his cigar again. 'They were on my trail just six months after I got the papers, but I did not return the papers to them. They even entered my residence secretly, but they could not even get a whiff of the papers. Now this is their last move, that is, they have started sending these death threats. It means they will kill me.'

'Okay. So did you ever see that Chinese man who handed you these papers again?'

'Never. I never saw him again.'

There was silence for some time and then Imran muttered, 'You will stay alive as long as those papers are in your custody.'

'Absolutely!' the colonel said with a surprise. 'You are really very intelligent. For this very reason, I don't want to return the papers to them. Think of it like this: I am holding a snake by its head; if I loosen my grip, it will definitely turn around to bite me.'

'Can I have a look at those papers?'

'Absolutely not! You are asking me to loosen my grip on the snake.'

Imran laughed, and then asked, 'Why did you involve Captain Fayyaz in all this?'

'Not even his ghosts have an idea what's really going on. He only knows that I am facing some threats but for some reason cannot let the police get involved in all this.'

'Then you shouldn't have told me all this,' said Imran.

'True, but it seems you have the devil's soul inside of you!'

'Imran's!' Imran said seriously. 'In any case, you

have invited me here as a bodyguard.'

'I wouldn't have invited anyone. This is all Sophiya's doing. She knows everything.'

'And your nephews?'

'They don't know anything!'

'You must have said something to them?'

'Just this—some enemies are on the lookout for me and the monkey is their insignia.'

'But what is the meaning of these all-nighters with loaded rifles? Do you think they will attack you when you expect?'

'I do this to distract the children.'

'Whatever—let's forget about it now.' Imran shook his shoulders. 'I prefer lemon drops and sugar cakes with my morning tea.'

Chapter 4

THE FOLLOWING MORNING SOPHIYA was surprised to see that her father was treating the mad man very differently from the previous night.

Anwar and Arif had their breakfast in their rooms: this had to do with the colonel's obsession with vitamins. If they ate with him, they would be forced to eat vegetables and chickpeas soaked in water and for this reason, they had started waking up late. These days they had found a good excuse because of the night patrol.

So today it was Sophiya, Imran, and the colonel at the table, and it seemed Imran was more 'vitamin-ized' than even Colonel Zargham. While the colonel was just eating the soaked chickpeas, Imran was peeling the skin off the chickpeas and piling it separately. Sophiya watched him with astonishment. When there was a considerable amount of peelings on his plate, Imran started chewing them.

Sophiya burst out laughing. Imran had not paid any attention to others around him till now, but when Sophiya laughed, a little smile flitted across his face. He looked up now at both of them, one by one, but continued the charade.

'I think you are eating the wrong thing,' Sophiya said, trying to suppress her laughter.

'Hain!' Imran said, his eyes popping out. 'Eating wrongly?' Then, acting startled, he began scratching his ears with his hand as if he had been eating through them. Sophiya's laughter increased.

'I mean, I mean you have been eating the peelings...' she said.

'Oh, I see, I see.' Imran laughed and shook his head. Then he said seriously, 'My health is worsening by the day; for that reason, I only eat that part of the meal which is just vitamins. These peelings are full of vitamins. Therefore I only eat them. Potato peelings, onion peelings, wheat peelings, etcetera, etcetera.'

'You are such a devil!' the colonel laughed. 'You are making fun of me!'

Imran started slapping his face. 'Aray! May God forgive me! What are you saying?'

Colonel Zargham was laughing uncontrollably. Sophiya was astonished. If someone else had dared to mock him, the colonel would have drawn his rifle at him in anger. She stared at Imran, then the colonel, then Imran again, and then the colonel, who was trying to draw Imran's attention towards the delicious dishes on the table.

'Are those two donkeys still sleeping?' Suddenly the colonel turned to Sophiya.

'Yes...'

'I am sick of them! I don't understand what they will grow up to be!'

Sophiya didn't answer. The colonel went on muttering to himself.

After finishing his breakfast, Imran came out of

140

the house. Sunlight had spread over the mountains. Imran gazed at them absorbedly. Sonagari's verdant green mountains were quite populated in the summers. The wealthy from surrounding areas usually retreated there to escape the heat. Hotels were full and even the smaller dwellings of the locals became the envy of paradise. The locals usually rented out their houses in summer and moved out into make-shift huts themselves. They also made a considerable income by serving as servants to their tenants. With this extra income, their winters were spent with reasonable ease and comfort.

Colonel Zargham had permanently settled there and he was considered one of the most influential people of the area. Sophiya was his only child. Anwar and Arif usually spent their summer holidays with him.

Imran stretched and began to look around him. The sweet smell of mulberries pervaded the whole place. The area where he stood was not an orchard, but it could have easily been one. Apricot, peach, apple, and mulberry trees were everywhere around him. The mulberries that had dropped on the ground had been rotting since God knows when, and the smell was unpleasant.

Imran had hardly turned to go back inside when he saw Sophiya approaching. He paused.

'Are you a private detective?' Sophiya asked as soon as she reached him.

'Detective?' Imran asked with a surprised expression. 'Not really. I don't think in our country there is such a thing as a private detective.'

'Then what are you?'

'Me?' Imran said seriously. 'What am I? Ghalib has composed a couplet for me:

I am bewildered: should I weep for the heart, or beat my chest for the liver? If I could, I would keep a hired mourner with me.

In reality, I am a mourner for hire. Those who have the means, hire me to beat out their hearts and liver. And I do it so efficiently, that they don't even have that...that thing...to feel surprised...what's-its-name...chance! Yes, chance! I don't give them a chance to be surprised.'

'Why do you think others are fools?' Sophiya asked irritably.

'I don't think I have ever considered even a fool, a fool.'

'Weren't you leaving today?'

'Tsk tsk! I am sad to report that Colonel sahib has acquired my services to reassure and comfort him. By the way, I also have a side business of comforting and reassuring people.'

Sophiya became quiet, and then she said, 'So you understand the matter?'

'I often reassure people without even understanding,' Imran said with a gloomy expression on his face. 'Once upon a time, a man acquired my services. I comforted and reassured him all night but in the morning I saw that there were two holes in his skull: he could neither beat his liver nor cry out his heart.'

'I don't understand.'

'Yes, later on, two bullets were recovered from

those holes. Miracle, it was a miracle! Indeed, we live in times of miracles. Just the day before yesterday I read in the paper that in Iran an elephant laid chicken eggs.'

'You seem to enjoy tormenting others,' Sophiya said, making a face.

'Your house is quite amazing,' Imran said, changing the subject.

'But the question is, what can you do for Daddy?' asked Sophiya in annoyance.

'Reassure him...'

Sophiya was about to say something when the colonel's voice boomed out from the verandah.

'Aray...you're here!' He came closer. 'The train arrives at eleven. Where are those two donkeys? You should all go to the station. I won't be able to go.'

'Will he not go back?' Sophiya said, glancing at Imran.

'No!' Zargham said. 'Hurry up. It's already half past nine.'

Sophiya paused to look at Imran for a few moments and then went back inside.

'Are there any guests arriving?' Imran asked the colonel.

'Yes. My friends,' Zargham said. 'Colonel Dickson—he's an Englishman—and Miss Dickson, his daughter, and Mr Bartosz.'

'Bartosz!' Imran said. 'Is he from Czechoslovakia?'

'Yes, but why? How do you know?'

'Such names exist only in Czechoslovakia.'

'Bartosz is Dickson's friend. I have never seen him. He's a painter.'

'Will they be staying here for some time?'

'Yes. They might spend the summer here.'

'Will you mention the Li Yu Ka matter to them?'

'Absolutely not!' the colonel said. 'But why did you even think of such a thing?'

'Just like that. However, I am thinking of something else.'

'What?'

'Those people have tried just about everything, but they have been unable to get the papers from you. They cannot even kill you without getting the papers because the papers might fall into someone else's hands. But will you be able to deal with the death of your daughter or your nephews?'

'What is this nonsense!' Zargham said, his voice trembling.

'I'm right,' Imran said, shaking his head. 'Suppose they kidnap Sophiya and demand the papers in return? What would you do then?'

'My God!' The colonel closed his eyes and leaned against a pillar.

Imran stood quietly. The colonel opened his eyes and said in a dead voice, 'You are right. What should I do? I have never thought about this.'

'Don't send Sophiya to the station.'

'Now I cannot even send Anwar and Arif.'

'All right. Why don't you go yourself?'

'I cannot leave these people alone either.'

'Don't worry about that. I will stay here.'

'You!' The colonel looked at him as if he was a

blockhead. 'You? What will you be able to do in face of some danger?'

'Haha! Why not? Haven't you seen my air gun?'

'Serious, my boy. Be serious!' the colonel said, lifting his hand impatiently.

'Do you take Captain Fayyaz to be a fool as well?'

'Aaa...no...'

'Then you can go without fear. My gun can shoot everything from a sparrow to a deer.'

'Keep my revolver with you.'

'Goodness, no!' Imran started to slap his face. 'What would happen if it fires?'

Zargham looked at Imran for a few seconds and then said, 'All right. I will stop them.'

'Oh wait! One more thing,' Imran said and then whispered something in his ear. The colonel's face turned pale for a few seconds and then returned to its original colour.

'But!' he said after a while, licking his dried lips. 'I don't understand...'

'You can understand everything. Now please go...'

'Oh, but...'

'No, Colonel. What I am telling you is correct.'

'You have put me in a bind...'

'Doesn't matter. Now just go.'

The colonel went back inside. Imran stood there, rubbing his hands. Then a wry smile spread over his face.

Chapter 5

ANWAR AND ARIF WERE upset that the colonel had stopped them from going to the station. They had not met Colonel Dickson or his daughter before. Even Sophiya was miserable. She too had wanted to go to the station.

'You didn't go with Colonel sahib?' Arif asked Imran.

'No,' Imran said indifferently and sucked on his gum.

'I hear that Colonel sahib is very happy with you?'

'Yes. I entertained him with jokes all night.'

'But why were we asked to leave?'

'The jokes weren't meant for kids.'

'What did you just say? Kids?' Arif was suddenly annoyed.

'Yes, kids.' Imran smiled. 'Colonel sahib was telling me about the love affairs he had in his youth.'

'What nonsense...'

'Nonsense it was indeed!' Imran said seriously. 'During Colonel sahib's youth, it wasn't normal for girls to fall for soldiers; in those days they only fell for lovers.'

'What kind of a person are you?'

'Hain? So you still think that it is my fault?' Imran asked, surprised. 'Colonel sahib was telling me himself.'

Arif laughed. After a while he asked, 'What about that monkey?'

'It was a good one.'

'May God look after you,' Arif said in an annoyed tone and walked off.

Strolling, Imran came upon the room where Anwar and Sophiya were playing chess. He stood quietly and observed them. Suddenly Anwar checked Sophiya. She moved her King to another square. From the other side, Anwar checked Sophiya again with the Bishop. Sophiya was about to make another move to save her King when Imran interrupted, 'Unhunh...Put it here!'

'What!' Sophiya snapped. 'Do you even know how to play chess or are you just...the King cannot move more than a square.'

'Is it a King or an earthworm? Kings can do whatever they please. This game is flawed. The Knight jumps two-and-a-half squares, the Bishop can go as far as it wants on his diagonals, the Rook runs from one end to the other in straight lines, and the Queen can go wherever she pleases—no questions asked! The King, it seems, is worse off than even the Knight. Shouldn't we call it a donkey for crawling from one square to the next?'

'Yaar, you are really some Plato!' Anwar laughed.

'Come on, make your move.' Sophiya was angry.

Sophiya played without thinking, and so she lost

soon. To tease her, Anwar began to laugh. Without paying him any attention, Sophiya turned to Imran. 'Why did you let Daddy go alone?'

'Because I don't go anywhere unarmed,' Imran said.

'What does that mean?'

'I was telling him I will take my air gun along, but he didn't agree,'

'Do you really shoot flies with your gun?' Anwar asked with an impish smile.

'Sir!' Imran placed his hand on his chest and bowed. Then, standing upright, he said, 'During the last World War, I almost won the Victoria Cross. My duty was to shoot down flies in hospitals. One day it so happened that a fly was sitting on the doctor's nose, and I missed my target marginally. To be honest, it was not my fault but the fly's: it flew off from the nose and sat on the eye. In any case, after that accident, all my earlier hard work was drowned in soda water.'

'Soda water!' Anwar laughed. Sophiya broke into laughter as well.

'Yes, clean water wasn't easily available in those days. Otherwise I would have said my hard work drowned in water.'

'You seem like an interesting person,' Sophiya remarked.

'I still claim that I am a great marksman.'

'Prove it to us, please,' Anwar said.

'Right away!'

Imran took out his air gun and loading a pellet, he said, 'Tell me which fly?'

A number of flies could be seen on the wall. Anwar pointed to one of them.

'Tell me the distance to shoot from,' Imran said.

'Go to the very end of the room.'

'Very well.' Imran moved in that direction. The distance was at least eighteen feet.

Imran took aim and pressed the trigger. The fly stuck to the wall. Sophiya ran to check and then turned towards Anwar with an astonished face. 'Really! This is amazing! Daddy's aim is pretty good but I doubt if even he could...'

'Oh, what's the big deal?' Anwar said pompously. 'I can do it too.'

He took the gun from Imran and soon even Sophiya joined the game. The plaster on the wall was being destroyed, but all of them had become obsessed. Arif joined them as well. The game went on for a while but no one succeeded. Suddenly Sophiya muttered, '*La haula wala quwwat!* What idiocy! The walls are ruined.'

All of them began to giggle, except for Imran, who had a serious expression on his face.

'True, the walls are destroyed,' Arif said. 'Colonel sahib will bury us alive.'

'This is all because of you.' Anwar pointed to Imran.

'Why because of me? I only shot a single fly!'

Anwar laughed. Then he placed his hand on Imran's shoulder and said, 'Yaar, please tell me the truth: are you really such a fool?'

Imran nodded gloomily.

'But last night you said something about the illegal drug trade?'

'I don't remember,' Imran said, acting surprised.

'Then why did Colonel sahib ask us to leave?'

'You should ask him.' Imran pointed to Arif, who started to laugh.

'What is it?' Anwar asked Arif.

'Aray, nothing. Nonsense,' Arif said, laughing.

'But what happened?'

'I will tell you later.'

Sophiya was staring at Imran.

'What about the monkey?' Anwar asked Imran.

'It was pretty good. A wonderful work of art.'

'What nonsense! Have you eaten grass or what?'[1] Anwar was annoyed.

'It is quite possible that we'll get grass for lunch,' Imran said with an innocent face. 'During breakfast I was given chickpea peelings.'

All three of them laughed out loud, but Sophiya soon grew serious and said in an angry tone, 'I know you were trying to make fun of my dad. I don't know why he didn't say anything.'

'It's quite possible he recalled that I own an air gun...' Imran said seriously. 'And frankly speaking, I was not trying to make fun of him. Even I care a lot for vitamins. When I see vitamins in peril, I see my nation in peril.'

'What's this you are talking about?' Anwar asked Sophiya.

'Nothing,' Sophiya said, trying to brush off the

---

[1] *Ghas khaana*: literally, to eat grass; figuratively, to lose (one's) wits or senses.

150

matter, but Anwar grew adamant. Finally Sophiya relented and recounted the whole story. A gale of laughter erupted.

'Yaar, you are amazing,' Anwar said.

'It is the first time I am hearing this. My father considers me a complete buffoon.'

'Then your dad himself is a...'

'Arrr...' Imran said, raising his hand. 'Please don't say that. He's a very important man: Director General of the Intelligence Bureau.'

'What?' Anwar said, his eyes popping out. 'You mean Rahman Sahib?'

'Yes,' Imran said indifferently.

'Aray, so you are *that* Imran who busted that American gangster McLawrence's ring!'

'I don't know what are you talking about,' Imran said in a surprised tone.

'No, no! You are the same person!' Anwar's face paled. He turned to Sophiya and said in an embarrassed tone, 'We have been making fun of a very formidable person.'

Sophiya was looking at Imran in utter astonishment. Imran let out his foolish laughter. 'I don't know what you all are harping on about.'

'No, Sophi!' Anwar said. 'I am right. A friend of mine, Rashid, was at Oxford with him. He told me about the McLawrence incident. After clashing with Imran sahib, McLawrence was destroyed along with his whole gang.'

'Someone has spread quite a rumour!' Imran smiled.

151

'McLawrence's head was smashed in two pieces,' Anwar said.

'Goodness!' Imran started slapping his face. 'If that's true then may my grave be visited by shyness...no...byeness...bananas...What do you call that little animal which enters graves...'

'Hyenas!' Arif said.

'May you live long. Yes, hyenas, hyenas.'

'Imran sahib, I want to apologize.'

'Aray, someone has misled you.'

'No, sir. I am sure.'

Sophiya was listening quietly and staring at Imran. Eventually she gulped and said, 'I think once Captain Fayyaz also mentioned you...'

'He might have. I strongly dislike that man. Last year he borrowed some five and a half rupees from me which he has not returned to this day.'

Chapter 6

AT QUARTER TO TWELVE, Colonel Dickson along with his daughter and Mr Bartosz entered the house. Colonel Zargham, however, was not with them.

Dickson was a lean, middle-aged man with light-blue eyes. The lower part of his moustache had turned brown due to excessive smoking. His young daughter was very attractive and when she laughed, little dimples appeared on her cheeks.

Bartosz was a heavily built, dashing man. In fact, it wouldn't be entirely inappropriate if he was simply called posh. A stylish beard complemented his face. His complexion was pallid, but his eyes radiated power. If it were not for these powerful eyes, he could have easily been mistaken for a liver patient.

'Hello, baby,' Dickson said, patting Sophiya on the shoulder. 'Are you well? I was expecting you all to come to the station.'

Dickson's daughter embraced her before Sophiya could reply. Then began the introductions. When it was Imran's turn, Sophiya hesitated a little.

Imran stepped forward to introduce himself, 'I am Colonel Zargham's secretary. Ignorant, Mr. Ignorant.' He then started laughing in a very odd manner. Dickson shrugged his shoulders indifferently and looked around.

'Where is Zarghi?' he asked.

'What! Is he not with you?' Sophiya said with a start.

'With me?' Dickson said. 'No...'

'Didn't he meet you at the station?' Sophiya's face turned pale.

'No. Not at all!'

Sophiya looked at Imran, who winked with his left eye.

But Sophiya's anxiety did not lessen. Soon she found a moment alone with Imran. 'Where is Daddy?'

'I don't know!'

'And you are sitting here so relaxed?'

'That's right.'

'For God's sake! Please be serious!'

'Don't worry. I am responsible for the colonel.'

'I am going out to look for him.'

'Absolutely not. You cannot step out of the house.'

'But why?'

'It's the colonel's order.'

'You are a very strange man!' Sophiya lost her temper.

'The guests should not find out what's going on. Please let those two know as well.'

'They don't know about this matter,' Sophiya said.

'At least they know that the colonel's life is in danger, no?'

'Yes.'

'They shouldn't even mention that.'

'Oh Lord, what should I do?' Sophiya said, almost crying.

'For the sake of the guests, please relax,' Imran said calmly.

'May God deal with you! I am going to go mad.'

'Don't worry. There is nothing to be afraid of. The colonel is not in any danger.'

'Are you crazy?' Sophiya said, annoyed.

Imran nodded his head as though confessing his insanity.

Chapter 7

IT WAS EVENING AND Colonel Zargham had not returned yet. Sophiya did not know what to do. Dickson was constantly asking about him. A couple of times, he even wondered if 'Zarghi' had started feeling uncomfortable around his friends. But, if that was indeed the case, why didn't he tell them plainly?

Sophiya forgot Imran's instructions in the midst of all this confusion. One of the instructions was that Anwar and Arif must not speak about the present circumstances to the guests. Sophiya forgot to mention this to Anwar and Arif. When Arif committed that folly, Sophiya was not present. She was in the kitchen helping the cooks while Imran, standing next to her, chattered on.

Dickson and the rest were in the verandah. Anwar was discussing Raphael's paintings with Bartosz. Arif was showing his album to Dickson's daughter, Martha, and Dickson was standing outside looking at the wavering twilight on the mountain peaks. Suddenly he turned to Arif and said, 'I didn't expect this of Zarghi.'

Arif was in a cheerful mood. For some reason, he felt a sense of belonging with these people. (It's quite possible that some of it had to do with Dickson's pretty and spirited daughter.)

'Colonel sahib, this is a huge secret,' he said, closing the album.

'Secret...?' Dickson muttered and stared at him.

'Yes. He had been terribly upset for the last fifteen–twenty days. During this ordeal, most of the times, we had to stay up all night. He was afraid of something. He used to say, "Any moment now, something can happen to me..." and God knows why he wanted to keep it a secret.'

'It's quite strange! And you all are still sitting here so relaxed?' Dickson said, jumping up to his feet.

Bartosz and Anwar stared at him. Anwar looked at Arif as if he was going to eat him alive. Even though Anwar had not been explicitly warned by Sophiya, he understood that Colonel Zargham wanted to keep this a secret.

'Where is Sophiya?' asked Dickson.

'Probably in the kitchen.'

Dickson headed towards the kitchen. The rest of them remained outside. Sophiya was cooking something in a frying pan. Imran was standing close by.

'Sophi,' Dickson said. 'What's all this?'

'Oh,' Sophiya said, surprised. 'It's too hot in here, I'll be right out in a minute.'

'Don't worry about that...tell me what's the matter with Zarghi?'

Imran rolled his eyes like an owl.

'I too am worried...I don't know where he has disappeared.'

'Don't lie. Arif just told me...'

157

'Oh...that...' Sophiya gulped and glanced at Imran.

'Actually, Colonel sahib, all those stories are ridiculous,' Imran said.

'Even with Zargham's disappearance?' Dickson asked.

'He often does this. He vanishes for days. It's nothing special,' Imran said.

'I am not satisfied with this explanation.'

'Ah. Even Confucius once said the same thing...'

Dickson looked at him angrily and said to Sophiya, 'Come quickly. I will be waiting for you in the verandah.'

Dickson left.

'What a problem!' Sophiya muttered. 'What should I do?'

'You have brought this trouble upon yourself. Why didn't you caution Arif?'

'I was so stressed, I forgot.'

'I explained the situation to you, so why were you stressed? I even told you that I myself have sent the colonel to a safe location.'

'But I had to make up something to satisfy the guests—is that less of a stress?'

'Would they have died without this information? I strongly dislike both your cousins.'

'What do I do now? Arif is an idiot.'

'In any case,' Imran said, deep in thought, 'hurry up now. I don't want anything to be said about me to the guests.'

Both of them came out to the verandah. Anwar had blasted Arif in Urdu for his stupidity earlier and now they were sitting there quietly.

'Tell me everything,' Dickson ordered Sophiya.

'No one knows everything except the colonel,' Imran said.

'What was he afraid of?' Dickson asked.

'He was very scared of a wooden monkey.'

'What nonsense!'

'That's why I said, don't ask about everything. I suspect his mental condition,' Imran said.

'And you let him leave the house alone despite that?'

'His mental condition is perfectly sound,' Arif said.

'You are back with your nonsense again!' Anwar scolded him in Urdu.

Dickson stared at Anwar.

'You all seem very mysterious to me,' he said.

'These two are very mysterious indeed,' Imran smiled. 'They spent the day today shooting flies with this air gun.'

Martha burst out laughing upon hearing this.

'*You* look more mysterious to me,' Dickson said sarcastically.

'Indeed,' Imran said in a low voice. 'It was I who advised them to shoot flies.'

'Look, I will explain,' Sophiya said. 'I don't exactly know about the circumstances but one day Daddy received a parcel in the mail from some unknown person. A wooden monkey was found in the parcel and Daddy got worried. He paced around the house all of that night and in the morning he employed eight armed guards from among the locals who guarded the house each night. Daddy only told us he felt he was in danger.'

'And what did the monkey mean?' Bartosz asked. He had been quietly listening to their conversation.

'Daddy did not tell us anything. He became angry when we insisted.'

'But why did you try to hide this from us?' Dickson asked.

'On Daddy's orders. He said talking about it might increase the danger.'

'Very strange!' Dickson said. 'I am not sure I will be at peace staying in this house in such circumstances.'

'I think the danger was for the colonel only,' Imran said.

'You're a fool!' Dickson was annoyed. 'I am not talking about danger. I am worried for Zargham.'

'Confucius has said...'

'Don't mention Confucius as long as I'm here, you understand?' Dickson grew angrier.

'Okay,' Imran nodded his head like a dutiful and obedient child, and tore open a pack of chewing gum. Martha cracked up again.

Chapter 8

INSPECTOR KHALID WAS OPENING his mail. He was a well-built young man. Before this appointment, he was in the army, but after the War he had been inducted into the Intelligence Bureau. He was an intelligent man and so had faced no difficulty in the Bureau. He was well respected in the department for his work. His features were sharp but his face bore no relation to his hair which was cut like that of a hardened man; there was, however, no harshness in his manner.

He had hardly rested his back against his chair when the phone buzzed.

'Yes?' he said into the mouthpiece. 'Oh, all right. I will be right over.'

He left his room and walked to the room of his department's Deputy Superintendent. He pulled the curtain aside.

'Come in,' the DS said, pointing him to a chair.

Inspector Khalid took a seat.

'I have summoned you for a private task.'

'Yes.'

'I have to ask for a personal favour,' said the DS.

'Name it, sir.'

'I have received a personal letter from the Federal Department's Captain Fayyaz.'

'Captain Fayyaz...' Khalid said, thinking. 'Yes, I think I know him.'

'One of their men is here. They want us to assist him in every way possible. His name is Ali Imran and he is residing in Colonel Zargham's place.'

'He's here in connection with?'

'We will have to find this out from him. This is his photo,' the DS said, handing him a photo from the drawer for his table.

'Very good,' Khalid said, looking at picture. 'I will take care of it.'

'Good. Another thing,' the DS said, refilling his pipe. 'What is the progress in the Shifton case?'

'It is a constant headache,' Khalid said, drawing a long breath. 'I don't think we will have a breakthrough any time soon.'

'Why?'

'We don't even know if Shifton is an individual or a group. And all the people who have received threatening letters from them are not only alive but have not paid any money either. I think it could be someone who has done this to make mischief. Almost every important person in the city has received such a letter, in which a large sum of money has been demanded...'

'Is there someone who has not received such a threat?' The DS smiled.

'I doubt anyone is left,' Khalid said.

'Think a bit harder.'

'I doubt if there's anyone.'

'Colonel Zargham!' the DS said, still smiling. 'We

haven't received any such complaint from him, even though he is a very wealthy man.'

'Oh...!'

'And now try to understand this,' the DS said. 'Colonel Zargham did not report any such threat, and the Federal Department's Superintendent is asking us to help someone who is based in his residence. Do you see now?'

'Definitely, it is something important.'

'Very important,' the DS said, taking the pipe out of his mouth. 'I think you should personally see that man...what's his name...Imran.'

'I will certainly meet him. But I don't know who and what kind of a man he is...'

'At all events, you will find out when you meet him,' the DS said and turned to the papers on his desk.

Chapter 9

THE MOOD WAS GLOOMY at the dinner table. The party finished eating and went to the verandah for coffee.

'Sophi,' Colonel Dickson said, 'I say we should inform the police.'

'That would be my suggestion too,' Bartosz said. He spoke very little.

'What should I do?' Sophiya said, distressed. 'Daddy did not want to make this matter public. And he was against involving the police from the outset. Once he even said that we should not worry even if he disappears. He said he would return as soon as he was out of danger. But he strictly warned us against informing the police.'

Imran looked at her admiringly.

'Zargham has always chosen to remain mysterious,' Dickson said.

'Everyone here is mysterious,' Imran said, and turning towards Martha he began to laugh.

'To be frank, I have not understood you as yet,' Dickson said to Imran. 'I don't know how Zargham has appointed you as his secretary. He is a very short-tempered man.'

'I used to recite Confucian proverbs to him,' Imran said seriously.

'You have brought up that name again! Are you trying to irritate me?' Dickson said angrily.

'No, uncle!' Sophiya interrupted quickly. 'This is his habit.'

'It's a bad habit!'

Imran went on sipping his coffee calmly.

'He is MSc and PhD, sir!' Arif laughed.

'You have started your nonsense again!' Anwar ground his teeth.

'Let him speak. I don't mind. Confucius...arrr... no...' Imran said, and nervously covered his mouth with his hands. Martha and Sophiya, who were seated on the sofas, started laughing. At this, even Dickson laughed. Bartosz's face remained as impassive as it always was—without even a hint of a smile.

Suddenly they heard footsteps coming through the gate. Whoever it was headed towards them. They all strained their eyes in the darkness. It was quite dark at the edge of lawn, where the lights on the verandah did not reach. Then the legs became visible because the visitor had a torch turned on. As he came closer they could see him dearly. He was a stranger: a well-built man wearing a beige pinstriped suit.

'Excuse me,' he said, coming close to the verandah. 'I am sorry to interrupt. Is Colonel sahib around?'

'No,' Sophiya said quickly. 'But please sit.'

The man took a seat. Sophiya said, 'He's gone out.'

'When will he return?'

'We are not sure. He might return tomorrow or a week later.'

'Oh, this is unfortunate,' the stranger said and threw an uncomfortable glance over those who were present. His eyes paused at Imran. 'Where has he gone?' he asked.

'Unfortunately, he usually doesn't tell anyone his plans,' Sophiya replied. 'Please leave your business card; we will let him know as soon as he returns.'

'It is an urgent matter,' the stranger said, sounding disappointed.

'You can tell me about it,' Imran said. 'I am the colonel's private secretary.'

'Oh,' the stranger said, sitting up straight. 'That's good. Can I trouble you in private?'

'Is that all?' Imran said like a fool. 'I don't understand what you mean by troubling me in private? What kind of a trouble would it be? You aren't asking me to strangle someone, are you?'

'Oh, I meant to say, can you come with me separately?'

'I always walk with my legs separate from others. I have never walked with my legs tied to anyone.'

'Aray, sahib! I mean to say, can you come with me?'

'Oh, why didn't you say it like this before?' Imran said, getting up. 'Let's go.'

The two of them walked towards the gate.

'You are Mr Ali Imran?' the stranger asked.

'I am the colonel's secretary.'

'That's all fine. Look, I am associated with the Intelligence Bureau and my name is Khalid. We have received instructions from the Federal Department's Captain Fayyaz to help you in every way we can.'

'Oh, Fayyaz! Haha! He's a very great man—friend of friends. I didn't know he would write a letter to his department for such a trifle. Very nice!'

'But what is the matter?' Inspector Khalid inquired.

'Has he not...written...?'

'No.'

'Yes, what would he have written anyway. The thing is, Mr Khalid, I have a great passion for partridges— partridge eating and partridge fighting—and in this area, there is a ban on partridge hunting. He said he will get me the permissions.'

Khalid looked at Imran for a few moments with an astonished expression. 'Then why did you say you are the colonel's secretary?' he asked.

'What else could I have said? Oh, I see, you disapprove of my designation here. That's all right, Mr Khalid. Actually, the thing is that I came here as a guest but then I got this job. The colonel really likes me. I shoot flies for him all day with my air gun.'

'Sir, you are trying to play with me,' Khalid said, laughing, and then grew serious. 'Even though the matter here is very serious.'

'What matter?' Imran asked, surprised.

'Whatever may be the case. You seem to be very intelligent. I am very sure you are among Captain Fayyaz's most important men. Let me just ask you one question.'

'Please.'

'Did Colonel Zargham ask for help directly from the Federal Department?'

Imran looked at him with a start. 'Help? I don't understand?'

'Sir, look,' Khalid said. 'It is quite possible that you have been in the Bureau for a long time, but I'm a novice. I am sure you are my senior, and for this reason I am not capable of challenging you. So if you speak openly, I will appreciate it very much.'

'All right, I will speak openly, but first you must tell me: what is the nature of your business with the colonel?'

'Nothing! Except this...' Khalid said, thinking. 'Let me explain, since you are new to Sonagari. Since last month, we have been trying to locate a mysterious individual or group called Shifton, who has written threatening letters to the local wealthy people and demanded huge sums of money from them. If the money is not received, they will be murdered, the letters say. Everyone has reported these letters except...'

'Except who?' Imran said quickly.

'Except that we have not received any such complaint from Colonel Zargham.'

'So you want us to write you one?' Imran broke into laughter.

'Oh, please look. You are not trying to understand. The thing is: why has the colonel been left alone? And if he has received it, why hasn't he reported it?'

'Really, you sound like a smart man indeed,' Imran remarked sarcastically. 'All right, suppose the colonel has also received a threatening letter. Is it absolutely necessary that he informs your department? It is quite possible he might have treated it as a joke. And even if he did not consider it a joke, there are many people who have little trust in anything except their own strength.'

'I only wish to know if he has received any such letter or not.'

'I cannot say for sure,' Imran said. 'I know nothing about it.'

'Why has Captain Fayyaz sent you here?'

'Because my brain has cracked open inside my skull. For this reason, cold air suits me in hot weather.'

'Oh, so you won't tell me anything. In that case, thank you for taking all the trouble. I will have to wait for the colonel's return.'

'At all events, we will keep on meeting.' Imran pushed forth his hand to shake.

'Oh, absolutely!' Khalid shook his hand and left.

Imran returned to the verandah. Everyone was waiting impatiently for him.

'Who was that?' Sophiya asked.

'Intelligence Bureau's Inspector Khalid.'

'What?' Dickson said with an astonished expression.

'What was the matter?' Sophiya asked anxiously.

Imran recounted the whole incident. Everyone was looking at him surprised.

He asked Sophiya, 'Did Colonel receive such a letter from Shifton?'

'No.'

'This is what I thought too. Why wouldn't he mention such a thing to his dearer-than-life secretary?'

'Why didn't you mention the other thing to him?' Dickson asked.

'Never. How could I have done such a thing?'

'You really sound like a crackpot to me.'

'For sure. Confucius...er...no...it is actually my own proverb that the ideal servant is one who does not budge even an inch here or there from his master's orders.'

'To hell with you!' Dickson roared and got up.

Chapter 10

ON THE DANCE FLOOR of Jeffery's Hotel in Sonagari, Inspector Khalid stood observing the dancing couples. Along with him was his section DS.

'See, there he is,' Khalid said, pointing towards Imran who was dancing with Dickson's daughter, Martha.

Sophiya was there too, but she was not dancing.

'Really?' DS expressed astonishment. 'He seems young. Anyway, I have asked Captain Fayyaz about his designation. He's probably here because of Zargham's girl, Sophiya. Who is that bearded man with him?'

'Some guest—Bartosz—from Czechoslovakia and that is Dickson. His girl Martha is dancing with Imran.'

'Keep your eye on this Imran,' the DS said. 'Okay, I am off now.'

The DS left.

The dance was over soon. Imran and Martha returned to their table. Khalid observed them for a few moments, then he too left the dance floor.

Imran was in full form. In just two or three days, Martha had dropped all her formalities. It was in her nature. She had become such good friends with Anwar and Arif that it seemed as if they had known each other for years.

'You dance really well,' she said to Imran.

'Really?' Imran asked, surprised. 'If this is true, then I will dance continuously day and night. My dad is a great man. He will be very happy to know this.'

'Are you really such a fool?' Martha smiled.

'My dad thinks so.'

'And what does my dear child's mother think?'

'My mom is a specialist in rectification by use of her slippers. For this reason, she expresses herself on special occasions only.'

'I don't get it.'

'I am sure you wouldn't. In England, it is not common to express oneself with slippers.'

Martha was distracted by something Arif said. The waiter was bringing a tray of coffee for them, which also had a glass of orange juice. Sophiya had ordered the juice. The waiter was some distance away when a man bumped into him. The waiter stumbled but regained his balance, saving the tray from toppling over as well.

Imran was watching this whole scene. His lips parted a little and then closed again. He was observing the man who apologized and moved on. As soon as the waiter placed the tray on the table, Imran hit the orange juice glass and knocked it over.

'Oh, what the hell!' Imran said nervously, picking up the glass.

'It seems you have never been in decent company,' Dickson said to him, annoyed. Bartosz stared at him with a strange expression.

'I will get another one right away!' Imran said,

looking at Sophiya, and stood up holding the glass. Sophiya did not say anything though her face betrayed signs of displeasure.

Imran went up to the counter and asked for another glass. The waiter, in the meanwhile, had cleaned up the table. Imran returned with the glass. The orange juice had splashed onto Martha's skirt and Sophiya's shalwar, and both looked irritated. The evening had suddenly become tense and they did not feel like staying on for much longer. But the question was, how could they leave? The stains on the clothes were very prominent and could be seen clearly from a distance.

'I have always seen clumsy men like you ending in disaster,' Colonel Dickson said to Imran.

'Yes,' Imran nodded his head. 'I have experienced this as well. Once I ate lemon drops thinking they were arsenic poison.'

Despite her annoyance, Martha smiled.

'Then what happened?' Arif asked.

'A childbirth. And he called me uncle.' Then Imran said to him in Urdu, 'You are trying to be a wise guy but Martha will not ever fall for you.'

'What's this nonsense you've started?' Sophiya said angrily, because she understood what was being said.

Imran didn't say anything. He was thinking something and his eyes were wide open like that of an owl which had suddenly been thrust into a room full of light.

A little while later, all of them got up to leave.

The stains on Sophiya's shalwar were covered by her long top, but the ones on Martha's white skirt were clearly visible. She reached the station wagon somehow. Everyone cursed Imran.

The station wagon headed towards Zargham's house. The night was very pleasant and Martha was sitting near Anwar on the front seat. For that reason, Anwar was driving slowly.

Suddenly, on a deserted street, they noticed three policemen signalling the car to stop with their raised hands. Anwar stopped the car. One of them was a sub-inspector and the other two were constables. The sub-inspector came forward and said, 'Turn on the lights inside the car.'

'Why?' Imran asked.

'We have received information that there is an unconscious girl in the car.'

'Haha!' Imran laughed. 'For sure, for sure.'

Anwar turned on the light inside the car and the inspector peered at everyone, straining his eyes in the dim light. Imran observed him with interest.

'Where is she?' Inspector thundered.

'Am I not unconscious?' Imran said, putting his finger on his nose and moving his body in an effeminate manner. 'I am unconscious! Why else would I be wearing a man's clothes! Oh please, go away...'

Sophiya, Anwar, and Arif all laughed out aloud.

'What is this nonsense!' said the sub-inspector, annoyed.

'Can I ask you from where you received this information?' Imran said.

'Nothing. Go now. It must be some other car.' The sub-inspector moved away. The car set off again.

Martha, who couldn't understand the conversation in Urdu, asked the reason for Sophiya's laughter, but she cracked up again.

'God knows what kind of a man is he!' she said.

She expected Imran to reply, but he was silent. He seemed absorbed in thought.

It was not very late, so on reaching home all of them busied themselves in some recreational activity or the other. Anwar and Bartosz played billiards. Dickson and Arif were waiting for Sophiya and Martha to play bridge; they had gone to their rooms to change.

Some time later, Imran knocked at Martha's door.

'Who is it?' Martha asked from inside the room.

'Imran, the great fool.'

'What's the matter?' asked Martha, opening the door. She had changed her skirt.

'I am sorry your skirt was ruined because of me.'

'Not a problem.'

'Oh no. Please give it to me. Otherwise the stain will become permanent.'

'Oh no, please don't worry about it.'

'Please, otherwise I will feel even worse.'

'It is impossible to get away from you.'

After some argument, Martha finally handed over the skirt to Imran. Next, he went to Sophiya's room. He had Martha's skirt in one hand and in the other, a bottle of milk.

'What is this?' Sophiya asked, surprised.

'I am going to remove this stain. Give me your shalwar too.'

'How absurd! Imran sahib, sometimes you irritate me very much.'

'No, please give it to me. I will not touch it with water. I will clean it with milk.'

'Do whatever you please. I don't care,' Sophiya huffed.

Imran picked up the shalwar, which was hanging from the side of the chair.

Sophiya watched him with an irritated expression. He poured the milk in a large bowl and started rubbing the stains into it. After a little while, the stains vanished. Sophiya's long-haired Persian cat had been repeatedly leaping for the bowl and Imran kept moving it away from the cat. When he was done with his job, the cat sprang onto the bowl. Imran did not stop it this time.

'Why couldn't you wash it with water? Why do you like exhibiting your foolishness so much?' Sophiya remarked.

'Hain? Have I committed some folly?' Imran said with a surprised look.

'For God's sake, don't bore me,' Sophiya snapped.

'Eve said the same thing when Adam hesitated to go near the forbidden tree.'

Sophiya did not reply. She was looking at the cat, which had fallen onto its side after lapping up the milk.

'Hain? What has happened to her?' Sophiya said, getting up.

'Nothing.' Imran lifted the cat by its leg.

'What happened to her!' Sophiya cried out.

'Nothing. She's just unconscious. God willing, she will regain consciousness before morning.'

'What in the world are you up to?' Sophiya said aggressively.

'They were fake policemen. They were supposed to find an unconscious girl in our car. Except, in that case, I wouldn't have been able to hang the girl like this,' Imran said, lifting the cat higher by its leg.

'What!' Sophiya said, her eyes growing bigger. 'You mean, these stains...'

'Obviously. They are not stains of Amrit Dhara.'

'But what does it mean...'

'Your abduction. I didn't let it happen.'

'You toppled the glass deliberately?'

'Yes.' Imran nodded his head and put the cat to the ground. 'Sometimes, I do commit such follies.'

'But how did you know?'

Imran recounted the tale of the man bumping into the waiter. 'My left eye is always open. I saw him putting something in the drink.'

Sophiya began to look scared. Imran said, 'Oh, please don't be frightened. But you will have to follow what I say at all times.'

Sophiya did not say anything. She was staring at this most foolish wise man in utter astonishment.

'And yes, please don't mention this incident to anyone,' Imran said, pointing to the unconscious cat. 'Not even to Arif and Anwar.'

'I won't, Imran sahib. You are indeed great!'

'I wish my dad would think the same way,' Imran said gloomily.

Chapter 11

INSPECTOR KHALID PICKED UP the receiver hastily.

'This is Khalid,' he said into the mouthpiece. 'Can you give me an appointment urgently? Thank you. I will come right away.' He quickly replaced the receiver and left the room.

The attendant at the DS's office lifted the straw curtain and Khalid went inside. The DS made a gesture with his head for him to sit. Taking the pipe out of his mouth, he leaned forward.

'Colonel Zargham's matter has gotten worse,' Khalid said.

'Why? Something new has happened?'

'Yes, and something very important. I tried to extract some information from the colonel's servants, and eventually one of them revealed that the colonel had not gone anywhere but has suddenly disappeared.'

'Good!' the DS said, emptying his pipe in the ashtray. Then he looked into Khalid's eyes.

'He went alone to receive his guests at the station but never returned from there.'

'Very good!' the DS tapped his finger on the table and then said, 'His family must be worried?'

'Absolutely not! And this is precisely what is so surprising.'

'Ahem.' The DS spread his legs and took a long stretch. He leaned back on the chair. 'Then, what do you think?' he asked a few moments later.

'I haven't reached any conclusion, sir.'

'Is it such a difficult problem?' The DS smiled. 'Colonel Zargham must also have received threats from Shifton. But then he disappeared. He did not inform the police. Others did and they have not been harmed. Think along these lines.'

'I have already thought on those lines.'

'And still you haven't reached any conclusion?'

'No, sir.'

'Strange. It is a very clear signal.'

'Please guide me. I am, as they say, a novice. I have to learn from you,' Khalid said.

'Look here. You write letters to two men: One of them knows you and the other doesn't. Suppose you write with your current designation saying that they are in danger and can be arrested any moment. The man who doesn't know you would think it is a joke, and would think someone has played a prank on him. But what would be the effect on the second one who knows you and is aware of your designation?'

'He will be startled,' said Khalid.

'Correct. Take this Shifton issue. Even for us, this name is new, let alone those who have received the letters. The colonel has not come to us with a complaint, which means he knows Shifton, and his disappearance like this means that Shifton is very dangerous. So dangerous that even the police cannot do anything to him.'

179

'As for me, I was wondering if he was Shifton himself!' Khalid said.

'If he is Shifton then there is no doubt that he is a fool,' the DS replied. 'If he was Shifton, he would have certainly come to us. No, Khalid, he's not Shifton. Otherwise he wouldn't have disappeared like this.'

'Then what should I do?'

'Look for Colonel Zargham.'

There was silence for a while, then the DS asked, 'What about Imran?'

'Nothing. His personality is also quite mysterious.'

The DS began to laugh and then said, 'Captain Fayyaz has replied to my telegram. Regarding Imran, he has written that he is a fool of the highest order. He's Fayyaz's friend. He has come here for entertainment. Often he invites troubles for his foolishness and for that reason Fayyaz wrote a letter telling me to help him in any such case.'

'But sir, how did he become Colonel Zargham's private secretary?'

'I don't believe Fayyaz's story too,' the DS said. 'These Federal guys never tell us anything openly.'

A heavy silence fell over the room.

Chapter 12

BECAUSE OF THE GUESTS, Arif and Anwar had to sleep in a single room. This room was next to Sophiya's and there was a door in between. Imran made a proposal to Arif that he knew Arif would agree to immediately. His proposal was that Arif should stay in Imran's room while Imran would move in with Anwar, replacing Arif. Arif was all too happy at this suggestion because Imran's room was next to Martha's. Anwar was very surprised at this change. He wished that Imran had switched rooms with him instead of Arif.

'But why did you leave that room?' Anwar asked him.

'I was having terrible nightmares,' Imran said seriously.

'Nightmares!' Anwar exclaimed in surprise.

'Ahan. Why not? I am terrified of English girls.'

Anwar began to laugh, but there was no change in Imran's serious expression.

After a while, Anwar said, 'But you haven't done the right thing by sending Arif there.'

'Okay, so why don't you go instead?'

'I...I didn't mean that,' Anwar stuttered.

'Then what do you mean?'

'Arif doesn't think before doing anything.'

'Hain? So have I sent him to do something?'

'I don't mean that...the thing is...'

'Then tell me what you mean, na...'

'I hope he doesn't do something...'

'What something?' Imran's eyes grew bigger.

'Oh, do you even understand or are you just acting again? I mean to say, I hope he doesn't make any advances towards her...'

'Oh, I understand,' Imran said in a serious tone, shaking his head. 'But what is the problem in advancing? There would have been a problem if he was retreating...'

'Making advances is just an idiom, Imran sahib!' Anwar said in annoyance, slapping his thigh.

'I don't understand,' Imran said foolishly.

'Uffoh! I mean to say I hope he doesn't make her fall for him...'

'*La haula wala quwwat!* Why didn't you tell me earlier?' Imran said, getting up.

'Where are you going?'

'I should alert Martha.'

'What are you talking about?' Anwar said, standing up. 'You are such a strange man.'

'Then what do you want?'

'Nothing. Nothing at all,' Anwar said, slapping his forehead with his palm.

'Yaar, you should get your brain checked,' Imran said angrily, sitting down. 'Why did you waste my time when there was nothing at all?'

'Come on, go to sleep,' Anwar said, falling on the bed. 'May God deal with you.'

'No. God should deal with you instead and then explain to me how to deal with you in a language I understand! I don't understand what you are talking about.'

Anwar pulled the sheet over his face.

Imran settled comfortably into the chair. Anwar was trying to sleep but who could sleep in such a state! The thought of Arif telling jokes to Martha and making her laugh was driving him mad. Martha was talkative herself and she liked people who could talk nonsense to her. Anwar's biggest problem was that when he thought too much about a girl, he was unable to talk to her openly. These days, Martha wholly occupied his mind, and he was unable to speak to her without stammering. He turned towards Imran, taking the sheet off his face.

'But where is Colonel sahib?' he asked Imran.

'Ahan! You did take your time in noticing that,' Imran smiled. 'I think he has run into some kind of an accident.'

'What?' Anwar sat up.

'Oho, it is not the kind of accident to get you worried.'

'Look, Imran sahib! Now this matter is becoming intolerable. Tomorrow, I will report him missing. I don't care.'

Imran didn't speak; he was in some deep thought. Anwar was on muttering, 'Colonel sahib has become old. I even doubt the soundness of his mind.'

'Yes, so what will your report be?' Imran asked.

'That Colonel sahib was afraid of some unknown

person or some group and suddenly went missing.'

'Ahan, and how will you explain the delay in reporting the event?'

'No big deal. I will tell them since we were afraid of Colonel sahib, it took us some time to decide to report it. He was against reporting the case to the police.'

'All right,' said Imran. He thought for a bit and then said, 'Go ahead and report it.'

Anwar looked at him in utter surprise.

'But,' Imran said, 'you will not mention a word about me. Understand? I am simply the colonel's private secretary.'

'Are you serious now?'

'When am I not serious?'

'But why have you now decided to file the report?'

'Necessity. Circumstances are always changing.'

'I don't understand what you want to do.'

'Ha!' Imran said with a sigh. 'I want to build a little bungalow, have a beautiful wife, and a dozen and a half kids.'

Anwar, annoyed, pulled the sheet over his face once again.

Chapter 13

IMRAN WAS SURPRISED TO see the serious-faced Bartosz on his knees. Bent over, he seemed to be smelling some plant. Bartosz noticed Imran and stood up, brushing his clothes. He smiled and said, 'I am obsessed with herbs.'

'Really?' Imran said in amazement. 'Then you must be aware of that herb which makes a man bark like a dog.'

Bartosz smiled. He said, 'I don't think I have heard of such a herb.'

'Quite possible. But I have heard of it. I love herbs.'

'Oh!' Bartosz was surprised. 'If this is true, then you can certainly help me.'

'Help?' Imran said, looking at him searchingly.

'Yes, I came to Sonagari in search of a herb. If I can find it...'

For the first time, Imran noticed that passive look leaving his face. His flat eyes revealed a spark and for a moment his face seemed as ebullient as a child's.

'If only I could find that herb!' Bartosz cleared his throat. 'I have heard that it is found in large quantities in a nearby area.'

'But what is so special about it?' Imran asked.

'Not now...not now, I will tell you later.'

Imran thought for a while and then said, 'Is it used for making gold?'

'Ah, you figured it out.' Bartosz laughed.

'How do you recognize the herb?' Imran asked.

'There are only three leaves in the whole plant—of a small, round type.'

'We will definitely look for it,' Imran said, nodding his head.

They were not too far from the colonel's bungalow. Bartosz pointed to a slope about a furlong in length and said, 'We should begin our search from there. There are lots of long-leafed thorny bushes in that area.'

'But a few moments earlier we were looking for round leaves, weren't we?' Imran said.

'Oh, that's right. Actually that herb grows near long-leafed bushes,' Bartosz said.

Both of them began to climb down the slope.

'Where is Anwar sahib?' Bartosz asked.

'I don't know.'

'I know.' Bartosz smiled. 'He has gone to report Colonel Zargham's disappearance.'

'What?' Imran stopped in his tracks.

'Yes. That's what he told me.'

'Oh goodness, we're doomed!' Imran said, slapping his forehead.

'What is wrong with reporting it? I don't understand.'

'You will never understand, Mr Bartosz,' Imran said, sitting on the ground. He then held his head like a gloomy widow whose insurance claims have been rejected.

'You look very worried,' Bartosz said.

'Everything's ruined now, my dear Mr Bartosz!'

'What has happened?'

'Nothing,' Imran said in a full-throated voice. 'Now I think this marriage will not happen.'

'What marriage?'

'Colonel Zargham's marriage.'

'Please tell me clearly.' Bartosz stared at him.

'He was trying to get married without letting his daughter know.'

'Oh, then, then really...' Bartosz paused mid-sentence and thought for a few moments, then laughingly said, 'I think the colonel must be an old man. Marriage in old age is an useless thing. Look at me, I have never married.'

'That's very good,' Imran said, nodding his head. 'I think we were going down in search of some kind of herb.'

'Oh, yes,' Bartosz said and began to move down the slope. When they reached the bottom, they began their search. Imran was showing unusual enthusiasm. It seemed as if this was his project and he was the one who had brought Bartosz along for help. They had come a long distance from the mansion and now some rocks blocked their view of the mansion.

'Mr Bartosz!' Imran said suddenly. 'We still haven't spotted a single rabbit. I don't think anyone keeps rabbits in this area.'

'Rabbits?' Bartosz said, surprised.

'It's useless. Let's go back,' said Imran. 'I should have thought about this earlier: there are no rabbits here.'

'We came here looking for herbs!' Bartosz said.

'Oh, *la haula wala quwwat!* And till now I was looking for rabbits,' Imran said, making a face.

In reality, however, Imran was not unaware of his surroundings. He had spotted three heads emerging from behind the rock on his right. Bartosz's eyes were flickering over the plants.

Suddenly, five or six men jumped out from behind the rocks and surrounded them. Their faces were covered with masks and two of them held revolvers.

'What is this?' Bartosz asked Imran nervously.

'I don't know,' Imran said, shrugging his shoulders indifferently.

'What do you all want?' Bartosz cried and leapt towards the men, but one of the men punched him on the forehead and Bartosz fell to the ground. He seemed unconscious.

'Come on, tie him up,' one of them said, gesturing towards Imran.

'Just a minute,' Imran said, raising his hand. He stared at Bartosz for a few moments and then said, 'I was lying. There *are* rabbits in this area.'

'What nonsense!'

'Yes, sir.'

'Tie him up!' the man called out to his accomplices again.

'Just a minute,' Imran pleaded. 'Let me note the time. I have to write a daily diary.'

He glanced at his wristwatch and then said in a disappointed tone, 'I am sorry, my watch is not working. You all should meet me some other time.'

Three of the men jumped at him. Imran took a quick step back and they bumped into each other. One of them regained his balance and leapt again.

'Aray, aray... What kind of a joke is this?' Imran said, head-butting the man's chest. The man fell on his back.

'Beware! I will shoot you!' Imran threatened the other two men advancing towards him as he drew out a fountain pen from his pocket. One of them laughed out loudly.

'Raise your hands,' the man with the revolver shouted.

Imran raised both his hands quietly.

One of the men drew out a coil of silk string and tried to bind Imran's hands. Imran placed the fountain pen on his right hand and suddenly the man let out a blood-curdling cry. Running back towards his two friends who held the revolvers, he snatched one of the guns and started shooting madly at Imran.

They all heard Imran cry out. He fell to the ground and began to roll down the slope.

'What have you done!' cried the man whose revolver had been snatched. He pushed aside the man who had shot at Imran and quickly went after him.

On reaching the edge of the rock, he looked below: he saw Imran's legs. The rest of his body was behind a big rock. The man climbed down swiftly. With one hand on the rock for support, he bent over the body.

But as soon as he bent down, the dead body seized his neck with both hands. The man struggled hard, but he could not get out of Imran's grip. Now Imran rose up in a sitting position. The other attackers had also reached the edge of the rock.

'Beware! Let him go or I'll shoot you,' one of the men shouted from up there.

Imran's prey was almost unconscious now; therefore he thought it best to use him as a shield.

'Go ahead. Shoot!' Imran said. 'But only on the condition that the bullet pierces through his chest to reach my liver. Otherwise, both of you should throw your revolvers here. If not, I will dispatch your friend heavenwards.'

The hands and feet of the masked man in his grip had grown limp; no one said a word from above.

Imran hollered again, 'All right, so I will end this story.'

'Wait!' someone shouted from above.

'For how long? I have never done such terrible business. I believe in taking with one hand and giving with the other.'

'Just shoot him,' someone else said. 'Don't worry about anything.'

Suddenly there was a gunshot. Someone had fired from the rocks in front. The masked men took cover and started returning fire. Imran left the unconscious man and took cover behind a rock that was out of range of fire. He was wondering who could be firing from the other rock. Had the news reached the house? Then he thought of Bartosz.

The exchange of fire continued for some time. Imran stayed behind the rock. Had he raised his head a little bit over the rock, the firing from either side would have certainly blown it to bits. The fountain pen was still pressed in his hand; it had a knife blade instead of a nib. Imran capped the pen and put it back into his pocket. Suddenly the sound of shooting stopped. There was silence for about three or four minutes. Then there was some firing from the rock in front, but the masked men did not respond. The gunshots were repeated a couple of times at short intervals, but there was still no response.

Imran crawled out from behind the rock and headed towards the spot where he had left the unconscious masked man. But he wasn't there. He heard footsteps behind him. He quickly turned and the next moment his face broke into a smile. The approaching man was Inspector Khalid.

'You aren't hurt, are you?' Khalid asked as soon as he reached him.

'Yes, I am hurt,' Imran said, making a face.

'Where?'

Imran placed his hand on his chest, 'Here. Because the contest was with a few veiled ladies.'

Khalid laughed and began to climb up. Imran was right behind him.

Above, they could not find anyone except for the unconscious Bartosz. There were plenty of empty cartridges from the revolvers. Khalid scrambled over the rocks and set off in search of the men. Imran stood with his eyes fixed on Bartosz.

'Such a long unconsciousness, my dear Bartosz?' Imran murmured and sat near him like a woman who had suddenly become quiet after grieving over her husband's dead body.

Khalid returned panting.

'They got away,' he said, sitting near Imran. After a while he said, 'Now you cannot deny it.'

'Deny what?' Imran said gloomily.

'That you know these men?'

'Oh, I've told you correctly, a few ladies...'

'Imran sahib!' Khalid raised his hand in protest. 'You are trying to mess with the law. Don't force us to take some measures against you.'

'Yaar, please have some tense...or whatever that idiom is,' Imran said, looking displeased. 'If I knew them, why would they come in veils? Wah! What's that line? "What a lovely veil, that you are visible through the screen."'

Khalid became thoughtful.

'How did you get here?' Imran inquired.

'I went to the mansion looking for you and found out you had come this way. When I reached here, I encountered all this and had to return fire.'

'Thank you,' Imran said seriously. 'But I don't understand something.'

'What?' Khalid stared at him.

'The distance between the mansion and here is not that much. Wouldn't the sound of the shooting reach there?'

'It would have certainly reached there.'

'And despite that, no one came here looking. Isn't it surprising?'

'It is, indeed,' Khalid said and stared at Imran curiously.

Bartosz moved a little a couple of times and then suddenly sat up, looking around with scared eyes. Then he jumped up.

'Those men...those men...' he stuttered, looking at Imran.

'Those men have dug up all the herbs and left with them,' Imran said with a sad face and then said, getting up, 'Now we must return.'

They all began walking towards the mansion. Bartosz limped along with his hand on Imran's shoulder.

'What happened to him?' Khalid asked.

'Herbalia,' Imran said.

Chapter 14

As they reached near the mansion, Imran flared his nostrils as if trying to sniff something. Suddenly he stopped and turned to Khalid.

'Can you smell something too?' he asked.

'Yes, there is something. Something sweet perhaps... this is the smell of rotting mulberries.'

'Absolutely not!' And saying this, he dashed towards the mansion. He entered from the back gate and immediately came out again. Meanwhile, Khalid and Bartosz had also reached the spot.

'What is it?' Khalid asked with a confused expression.

'Something's certainly wrong inside,' Imran said slowly. 'No, don't go inside. It's filled with synthetic gas. This sweet smell is of the gas.'

'Synthetic gas?' Khalid muttered. 'What is this thing anyway?'

'It temporarily paralyses your brain. I am sure no one inside will be conscious,' said Imran.

Suddenly they heard a cry and saw Dickson stumbling out from the back door. He was stamping his feet on the ground in great agony. His face had turned red and water flowed from his nose and eyes.

Khalid wanted to question him, but Imran interrupted him by raising his hand, 'We don't have time for this. We have to do something for those inside, otherwise someone might die.' Instructing Bartosz to wait and signalling Khalid to follow him, he charged off. They went around the mansion and came to the verandah. Here the smell was even stronger. Imran pinched his nose and stormed in. Khalid followed him, but after a few steps he began to feel suffocated. He was thinking of turning back when he saw Imran returning with someone on his back. Khalid moved aside and came out with him.

Dropping the unconscious Arif on the lawn, Imran said to Khalid, 'Yaar, have some courage. Can't you hold your breath for a few minutes? Their lives are in danger.'

Working very hard, they carried out all of them one by one—except Sophiya, who wasn't among them. Imran scanned the whole mansion, but there was no sign of her.

It took about two hours to bring them back to consciousness and to clear the air in the mansion. No one was able to tell them anything of use. No one had a sense of what had happened or how.

'Imran sahib!' Khalid said very angrily. 'Things have gotten out of hand. Now you have to explain the situation to me. The matter isn't so complex, I'm sure, that I won't understand anything. Where is the colonel's daughter?'

'Tell me if you have any idea. I don't know anything,' Imran said coldly.

'Either she has done this herself and fled, or someone has kidnapped her,' Khalid said.

'Shifton has taken her away,' Imran said.

'Then why did you have to waste all this time?' Khalid said, annoyed.

'What do you mean by wasting time?' Imran said dryly.

'When I asked you about Shifton, you expressed ignorance. Why did you mention his name now?'

'Should I have mentioned Emperor Baodani's name then?'

'Look, you are still making things complicated.'

'Yaar, who am I in the first place?' Imran jerked his neck. 'You are an official. You should note down our statements, give us some assurances. That some veiled ladies had attacked me—write that sad account as well, etcetera, etcetera...'

'I want to take you to my office,' said Khalid.

'Look, friend, I am not ready to waste my time.'

'Don't force me to take stringent action, please.' Khalid's expression turned harder.

'Really? Is it like this?' Imran said sarcastically. 'What can you do, sir? Has anyone in this house sought your help? Who are you to interfere in our private matters anyway?'

The others were lying silently on the sofas. No one had the physical strength to express his or her opinion. They were like a disinterested audience. Inspector Khalid threw an indifferent glance at them and said to Imran, 'Imran sahib, I have great regard for Captain Fayyaz, otherwise...'

Suddenly Bartosz interjected, 'What are you guys doing for the girl? It seems to be the doing of those same criminals.'

'Yes, my dear Mr Khalid,' Imran said, nodding his head. 'For now, we have to see where Sophiya has gone.'

Khalid did not reply. Imran came out into the verandah. Khalid followed him.

'It is a bad idea to build a mansion in an isolated area,' said Bartosz, who was standing at the door and looking around.

Suddenly Imran left the verandah and started walking. He paused near the rose bushes and bent down. A lady's black sandal lay there. Khalid and Bartosz also reached the spot.

'Oh, this seems to be that girl's...'

Imran didn't say anything. His eyes shifted from the sandal to something else. He turned to Khalid.

'You must know every nook and cranny of Sonagari, right?' he asked Khalid.

'Not just Sonagari, I even know the suburbs as well quite well,' Khalid replied, but his tone wasn't pleasant.

'Is there any such place here where the soil is red?'

Khalid thought for a few seconds and then said, 'Why do you ask?'

Imran picked up a piece of red clay that still contained a little moisture. 'I think,' he said, 'this clay was stuck in between someone's sole and heel; and I haven't seen soft earth anywhere around this area within a two-mile radius. Look at this, it is still a bit moist.'

Khalid took the clump in his hand to examin it.

'There is a place near Paltan Camp area where such soil can be found. Actually there is a small stream there as well. The clay by the banks of the stream is always moist.'

'Is it an isolated area?'

'We cannot call it isolated, but yes, it is sparsely populated. The upper classes generally reside there.'

'Can you take me there on your bike?'

'Possibly,' Khalid said, thinking.

'Then wait,' said Imran and went inside the mansion. He addressed Anwar who was lying on a sofa like an opium junkie.

'Listen! I am going in search of Sophiya. If you are unable to move, inform the police over the phone. Where the hell are all the servants?'

'They are all out today,' Anwar said in a weak voice. 'They left for the city in the morning, but they still haven't returned.'

It was the colonel's practice to allow his servants a half-day leave once each week. Imran stood thinking for a few seconds. Then he walked into the room where his luggage was kept. He took out a few things from his suitcase and, stuffing them into his pocket, walked out of the mansion.

Chapter 15

IT WAS A VERY pleasant day. Clouds had been drifting in the sky since dawn and hadn't let even a ray of sunlight escape their cover.

Inspector Khalid's bike was heading towards Paltan Camp. Riding pillion, Imran nearly dozed off. His face showed some nervousness. His foolish mannerisms had disappeared. Close to Paltan Camp, it began to drizzle and Khalid reduced the speed of his bike.

'But how are we going to find them when we get there?' Khalid asked Imran.

'Aha! A CID Inspector is asking *me* this?'

'Imran sahib, I expect some seriousness from you in such a situation.'

'Aha, some wise man has said: the world survives on hope. Is there a restaurant in this area where the locals hang out? If there is one, please take me there.'

Inspector Khalid turned his bike onto a narrow road but Imran immediately asked him to stop. Khalid hastily stopped the bike. This was a very open spot and cultivated land surrounded them on both sides of the road. They could see flower gardens on either side of the road. It was among the recreational spots of Paltan Camp.

Khalid paused and put his feet on the ground.

Suddenly he turned off the engine. He had seen a girl standing in the gardens, waving her handkerchief at him to attract his attention. Khalid got off the bike.

'Imran sahib, please wait.'

'Do you know her?' Imran smiled.

'Yes.' Khalid laughed.

'Very good, you may go. But the bike will stay here unguarded,' Imran said, glancing at the left side of the gardens. 'I will go over to the other side. My deloveb, deloveb...I think I am using the incorrect word...what do you call her who is loved?'

'Beloved.'

'Beloved...beloved! My beloved is on the other side. All right, so I will go now.' Imran got off the bike.

To his left, he had seen some faces that seemed familiar from the nightclub. Imran recognized one of them very well. It was the same man who had bumped into the waiter. He was unsure about the other two. He wasn't certain if they were the accomplices of that sub-inspector who had stopped them on that deserted road that night searching for an unconscious girl.

There were four of them. There was no woman with them. Imran began to talk about the cultivation of apples and apricots with the keeper of the garden.

Chapter 16

SOPHIYA LOOKED AROUND THE room with astonished eyes. She didn't know where she was. The room was luxuriously furnished and she was lying on a comfortable bed. She tried to get up but failed. She felt as if there was no strength in her body. Her mind wasn't working. She dozed off again. The clock on the wall struck eight when she opened her eyes the next time and the lamp on her bedside was turned on.

This time she sat up at the first attempt. For a while, she sat with her head in her hands, then she stood up. Her head was spinning so terribly that she had to grab the edge of the table to steady herself. The door in front of her was open. She was about to go out of the room when a man entered.

'Colonel sahib wants to see you,' he said very respectfully.

'What? Daddy!' Sophiya said, completely astonished.

'Yes.'

Despite her weakness, Sophiya moved swiftly, and the man had trouble trying to keep pace with her. After going through numerous corridors, they entered a large room. What Sophiya saw there was enough to leave her half-dead.

Colonel Zargham was tied to a chair and four

men surrounded him. They were looking at him fiercely.

'You!' Zargham shouted suddenly and tried to get up. But he couldn't move. He was tied very firmly.

Both of them stared quietly at each other.

Suddenly a man with a heavy jaw said, 'Colonel, you are trying to take on Li Yu Ka. Li Yu Ka, whom no one has ever seen ...'

Zargham did not say a word. His eyes shifted from Sophiya to the ground.

The man with the heavy jaw said, 'If you don't return those papers to us, your daughter will be chopped to pieces, bit by bit. Will you be able to watch her suffer like that?'

'No!' Zargham cried uncontrollably. Drops of sweat appeared on his face.

Sophiya stood trembling. Her head was spinning again. It seemed as if the light inside the room was obscured under layers of dust. The man who had brought her in caught her as she fell. She was unconscious again.

'Put her on the chair carefully,' the man with the heavy jaw said. He then turned to Zargham. 'If you still don't come to your senses, it will be unfortunate.'

Zargham stared at him for a few moments, then pursed his upper lip and said, 'Cut her to pieces! I am Colonel Zargham! You will not even see the shadow of those papers.'

The man with the heavy jaw laughed.

'Colonel, despite knowing Li Yu Ka's powers, you are talking foolishly,' he said. 'Didn't you see how

202

Li Yu Ka dug you up? You were hiding in a place where even angels wouldn't have dared to touch you. It was Li Yu Ka's powers that effected the kidnapping of your girl in broad daylight. I ask you: what use are those papers to you? Believe me, those are of no use to you. But you are a smart man—you did not turn those papers over to the police. Tell me, what do you want?'

'I don't want to answer any of your questions. Do whatever you want,' Zargham roared.

'All right,' the man with the heavy jaw said, pointing to one of his men. 'Cut this girl's big toe.'

The man lifted a shining axe and moved towards the unconscious Sophiya.

'Wait!' a voice thundered suddenly. 'Li Yu Ka is here!'

At that instant there was an explosion. A blinding light shone from the wall in front of them and the whole room was filled with smoke. Thick, white smoke. One couldn't even make out a thing at arm's length.

The furniture started toppling down to the floor. Colonel Zargham's chair also toppled. But he was alert enough to protect his head from hitting the ground. The men in the room raised a hue and cry, like dogs abruptly roused from a deep slumber. Suddenly the colonel found himself getting up from the chair and standing up. Someone held his hand and pulled him to one side. Zargham, because of the smoke, had lost his wits and had to be pulled along.

A short time later, he found himself in fresh air.

Above his head was the open, star-filled, sky. He tried to peer at the man who held his hand and was pulling him along the sloping ground. He was carrying someone on his shoulder, but despite the weight his feet were moving nimbly.

'Who are you?' Zargham asked in a hoarse voice.

'Ali Imran, MSc, PhD,' came the reply.

'Imran...!'

'Ssshh...come along quietly.'

Soon they reached a safe spot among the rocks. These rocks were such that one could stay hidden there for hours.

Imran took down the unconscious Sophiya and put her by a rock.

'Why? What happened?' the colonel asked.

'I have to have a chewing gum first,' Imran said, fumbling in his pockets.

'What a strange man are you! Aray, that building is not far from here!' the colonel said nervously.

'That's exactly why I have paused. So that I may see the spectacle. Is there a fire station nearby?'

'Why? Is that building on fire?' Zargham asked.

'Of course not! It would create a hoopla for nothing. It was a simple smoke bomb. Take a look at that smoke cloud.'

The colonel looked towards the building. Above the top floor floated a thick cloud of smoke.

'Did you...that bomb...?'

'Aray no...La haula...' Imran said, slapping his face. 'I mistook it for a tube of toothpaste. But I feel sorry for them because all the entrances of the building are closed. Last night I had a dream in which I was instructed that such things are to be expected as we near the end of the world, etcetera, etcetera.'

'Imran, I swear to God! You are a gem!' Zargham said passionately.

'Oh, don't say that, custom officers will levy duty on me,' Imran said. 'But how did you get trapped here?'

'I had taken refuge in a spot where no one could've reached me, but they got me out like a plagued rat.'

'Gas!'

'Yes! I was in a cave. They used a gas and I was forced to come out. But how did Sophiya get here?'

'Wait!' Imran raised his hand. He seemed to have heard something in the distance. He said hurriedly, 'I will explain later. Get up now, the cars have arrived.'

He tried to lift Sophiya again, but the colonel stopped him. He picked her up himself and then started following Imran. The descent was very steep, but they kept on moving carefully. Soon they saw a narrow winding road, clear in the starlight. Suddenly red rays of light spread on the rocks. The colonel cried out.

'Don't worry. It's the police,' Imran said.

Five or six men came up to help them. Among them was Inspector Khalid.

'That building is on fire,' he told Imran.

'Make arrangements to send these people there,'

Imran said. 'And you should come with me. Ten men will be enough.' He then turned to Zargham. 'You are weak. For the time being, don't give any statements to the police.'

'What does that mean?' Khalid said, annoyed.

'Nothing, dear. You come with me. Bring your men as well.'

'Everyone is already there,' Khalid said.

The colonel and Sophiya had been brought down the hill. Imran, along with Khalid, headed for the building again. Thick smoke rising from its windows was coiling in the air. A large crowd had gathered around the building. Khalid's men joined them and Imran entered the building with them. All the doors had been shut, and those inside could not leave.

There were certain rooms in the building where the smoke was less. They found all five men huddled in one such room. All of them were drenched in sweat and panting considerably.

'What is it?' Imran shouted at them as soon as he neared them.

Upon seeing him, their condition seemed to turn worse.

'Why don't you speak?' Imran thundered, but none of them spoke up. Imran turned to Khalid. 'They are Shifton's men. They were making smoke bombs, one of which exploded.'

'That's nonsense!' the man with the heavy jaw shouted.

'It doesn't matter,' Khalid said, jerking his neck. 'I arrest you for wrongful confinement.'

'That's such nonsense.' The man with the heavy jaw smiled. 'We have not kept anyone in wrongful confinement.'

'Yes, Khalid sahib!' Imran said, rolling his eyes foolishly. 'It won't work like this. They have probably destroyed all proof of wrongful confinement. No, these guys were making bombs.'

'Handcuff them!' Khalid ordered his men.

'Look, you are asking for trouble!' the man with the heavy jaw said in an annoyed tone.

'Don't worry,' Khalid said, drawing a revolver. 'Get handcuffed quietly now, otherwise you will meet an unpleasant end. I am the army type, you see.'

All of them were handcuffed. After they had been shifted to the police car, Khalid asked Imran, 'Now what charges should be brought against them?'

'Bomb making. People in the nearby areas must have heard the explosion. Recover a dozen kilos of sulphur and a couple of jars of acid. That should be enough.'

'And that Shifton matter?' Khalid asked.

'For now, not even your angels can provide any evidence for that. Okay, I will go now. At least don't let them out on bail.'

Chapter 17

THE FOLLOWING MORNING THE Intelligence Bureau's DS's car was parked in the compound of Colonel Zargham's mansion, and he was inside recording the colonel's statement. Imran had prepared Zargham thoroughly the night before. He regurgitated everything that Imran had taught him. He told the DS that he had also received a letter from a mysterious Shifton and he had disappeared because of his fear. Then answering a counter-question, he said he had been Shifton's target earlier as well and he had lost fifty thousand rupees then. But he was unable to say if Shifton was the name of an individual or an organization.

At all events, the colonel did not let the DS get even a whiff of the Li Yu Ka case or any of its details. About the previous night's events, he said Shifton's men were exercising force on them and demanding one hundred thousand rupees when there was an explosion. And because his secretary Imran was already in the area searching for Sophiya, he immediately came to their aid.

God knows if this satisfied the DS or not, but in any case, he didn't stay there for too long.

Sophiya was still traumatized. She asked Imran, 'Imran sahib, what will happen now?'

'Dancing, singing—everything. Don't worry,' Imran said.

'Did you really throw the bomb?'

'Aray, may God forgive me!' Imran slapped his face. 'Don't say such things, otherwise my mom will throw me out of the house!'

Sophiya was about to say something when the colonel called out to Imran from his room. Imran left Sophiya and went into the other room. Zargham was alone. When Imran entered, he closed the door.

'Look here.' The colonel pointed to the table on top of which there was a large dagger.

'Possibly another threat from Li Yu Ka?' Imran smiled.

'I swear to God you are very smart!' The colonel placed his hand on Imran's shoulder and said in a trembling voice, 'Yes, an open letter from Li Yu Ka. And that dagger. In this room. I wonder who brought them here.'

Imran stepped forward and picked up the letter. Below the text of the letter was the signature 'Li Yu Ka'. Imran read out the letter:

'Colonel Zargham! You are being given one last chance. Think about it. Otherwise by tomorrow evening one of your nephews will be murdered. You can hide them anywhere. If you don't come to your senses even then, you will see your daughter's dead body. If you are ready to return those papers, float a red balloon from your compound at five this evening.'

Imran looked at the colonel.

'Dickson wants to know the real story,' Zargham said. 'He doesn't believe the Shifton story. I can't understand who is Shifton and where he figures in all this.'

'Shifton,' Imran said, 'is nothing. Call it a little trick of Li Yu Ka. He has done this so that you would not seek police help. Think about it: every influential person in the city is complaining to the police about some Shifton and suddenly you ask for their help using this Li Yu Ka story. The result is clear: the police will consider both of them a farce. So instead of getting help, you would have got a response that someone was playing a prank on all the influential persons of the town. Am I wrong?'

'You are right,' the colonel said, thinking. 'But my mind is giving up now. I don't know what to tell Dickson. We have been such close friends for years. Nothing is secret between us.'

'I think you should tell him everything and all of us should gather in some place to consult over this. Let's gather everybody in one room.'

'How will this help?'

'It's quite possible we might find some good advice.'

'I sometimes think I should turn over the papers to the police,' Zargham said, rubbing his forehead.

'In that case you won't be able to get away from Li Yu Ka's vengeance.'

'That is what stops me,' Zargham said. 'But Imran, my son, I am very sure I won't stay alive even after returning the papers.'

'Not just you,' Imran said, thinking. Everyone who is helping you will be in danger.'

'Then what should I do?'

'Will you do as I tell you?' Imran asked.

'Yes!'

'Then be quiet. I will gather everyone except the servants for consultation. In the meanwhile, you can sing that movie song. What are the lyrics? Yes...*Dil le ke chale to nahin jao ge ho raja ji...ho raja ji!*'

'What nonsense!' Zargham said, annoyed. And then he broke into laughter.

Chapter 18

THAT SAME EVENING, AT about five, a red balloon rose up in the air from Colonel Zargham's compound. Everyone was present in the compound, their faces pale; only Imran was clapping and giggling like a child.

That afternoon, Zargham had recounted the story and everyone was of the opinion that Li Yu Ka was a dangerous man and that the papers should be returned. Dickson already knew his name—it wasn't new for Europeans. Li Yu Ka's trade was common knowledge in continental Europe as was the fact that despite the trade being cent percent illegal, no one had ever been able to get their hands on him. In fact, Dickson and Bartosz had turned pale the moment they heard Li Yu Ka's name.

Li Yu Ka's response came that very night, just before dinner. And its manner of arrival was as mysterious as the earlier message. Arif saw a dagger stabbed in the frame of a door. It held a piece of paper.

The colonel had been instructed to leave the papers in a crack of the famous Black Rock in Devgarhi—or ask someone else to do so on his behalf. It also said that he might bring along as many men as he wanted if he felt in danger. However, in case of fraud or deception, he wouldn't be forgiven.

On the dining table, a heated debate started about the letter.

'Is Li Yu Ka some kind of a ghost?' Martha said. 'How do these letters get here in the first place? It seems that Li Yu Ka is not a person but a spirit.'

'Yes, yes,' Imran said, nodding his head. 'It is quite possible. To be sure, it is some drug addict's spirit, which has started the drug trade even in the World of Spirits.'

'I have a suggestion,' Bartosz said to Colonel Zargham. 'But I don't think it is appropriate to mention it in front of the young ones.'

'Mr Bartosz, I hope you don't consider me a kid,' Imran said.

'You are the devil's grandfather himself!' Bartosz said, smiling.

'Thank you. I am happy that my nephews remember me at all times,' Imran said seriously.

Dickson stared at him. He was still under the impression that Imran was Colonel Zargham's private secretary, and he thought it was very insolent for a secretary to speak so casually to an honoured guest like Bartosz. But he didn't say anything.

After dinner, Sophiya, Martha, Anwar, and Arif got up to leave.

Dickson was waiting impatiently for Bartosz's advice.

'I am an artist,' Bartosz said in an unhurried tone. 'In such a situation advice is not expected from a person like me.'

'Mr Bartosz,' Colonel Zargham said, raising his

hand impatiently. 'Leave the formalities for another occasion.'

Bartosz thought for a few moments and then said, 'I have heard Li Yu Ka's name a lot and I also know that he personally participates in such expeditions. If the traditions I have heard about him are correct, he should be present in Sonagari at this time.'

'Okay,' Imran said, rolling his eyes.

'And if he's here, then we should definitely take advantage of it,' Bartosz said.

'I don't understand what you mean?' the colonel said.

'If we could capture Li Yu Ka, it would be a great service to humanity.'

Zargham laughed disdainfully, but there was more annoyance than disdain in his laughter. He said, 'You will capture Li Yu Ka? *The* Li Yu Ka? He can put us to death whenever he wants!'

'Tsk tsk,' Bartosz said, making a face. 'You are assuming that Li Yu Ka or any such man is bestowed with supernatural powers. No, my dear Colonel. It is my contention that someone from this house is working for Li Yu Ka.' And then, to render some weight to his argument, he banged the table with his fist: 'I claim there is no other way but this.'

A hush fell upon the room. Zargham stared at Bartosz, holding his breath.

'I agree with Mr Bartosz,' came Imran's voice. And a silence fell again.

Finally, Zargham cleared his throat and said, 'Who could it be?'

'Whoever it is!' Bartosz shrugged his shoulders indifferently. 'When it comes to Li Yu Ka, you cannot trust anyone.'

'You made a mistake, Colonel sahib,' Imran said to Zargham. 'You should have consulted Mr Bartosz much earlier. His information on Li Yu Ka seems very comprehensive to me.'

'Indeed it is! I know a lot about Li Yu Ka. There was a time when my life was spent among the most vulgar sections of society where criminals, thugs, and illegal drug traders were common. And it was then that I got to know much about Li Yu Ka. Colonel, you think Li Yu Ka will ask one of his men to get these papers from the rocks? Absolutely not! He will get them himself. No one knows Li Yu Ka or who he is. But what is there in these papers?'

'From what I could understand, there is nothing in there which could shed any light on Li Yu Ka's personality,' the colonel said.

'Wah!' Imran said, jerking his neck. 'How can you say this with such assurance when you don't know Japanese or Chinese?'

'Chinese and Japanese?' Bartosz fell into some thought. Then he said, 'Can you show me those papers?'

'Absolutely not!' Zargham shook his head. 'That is impossible. I will seal them in a packet and leave them where Li Yu Ka has asked me to.'

'You will be committing a grave crime against humanity!' Bartosz said passionately. 'It would be better to give yourself into police custody and hand over the papers to them.'

'Mr Bartosz, I am not a child!' Zargham said in an acerbic tone. 'The papers have been safe in my custody for a long time now. If I wanted to seek police help, I would have already done so.'

What was the point of keeping them with you for such a long time?'

'The point is clear,' Dickson spoke for the first time. 'Zargham is alive only because he still possesses the papers. If Li Yu Ka had gotten hold of them, Zargham wouldn't have been sitting here among us.'

'Okay,' Bartosz said, nodding his head reflectively.

'But what was your scheme, anyway?' Colonel Zargham asked impatiently.

'Wait, I will tell you,' Bartosz said and paused for a few moments. 'Li Yu Ka will come alone to that place. If we hide a few people there, then...'

'That's a good idea,' Imran said, nodding his head. 'But you have already said...Anyway, forget it...But who will bell the cat? Colonel sahib doesn't want to involve the police in the matter, and besides, it is not necessary that the cat would want to have a bell tied to its neck in the first place.'

'Show me the place, and I will tell you who will bell the cat,' Bartosz said stiffly.

All of them went quiet. Soon a whispered consultation ensued, and eventually it was agreed that they would go to examine the Black Rock of Devgarhi immediately. Colonel Zargham was reluctant, but seeing Imran's enthusiasm, he had to agree. He had now begun to trust Imran's foolishness.

The night was dark. Zargham, Dickson, Bartosz, and

Imran were proceeding to Devgarhi through difficult, winding roads. They had little torches in their hands, which they would occasionally turn on. Dickson, Zargham and Bartosz were armed, but Imran only seemed to have his air gun in his hand—and carrying an air gun does not qualify someone as 'armed'.

They stopped when they reached near the Black Rock. It looked quite frightening in the dark. Its structure was such that it looked like the mouth of a large, monstrous python.

Bartosz examined it for about half an hour and then said, 'It is very easy. Very easy. Look at these caves. Thousands of men can hide in them. We should make use of this opportunity.'

'One man would be enough for Li Yu Ka,' Imran said.

'I have never been able to understand what kind of a man you are,' Bartosz said, irritated.

'Have I said something irrelevant?' Imran said seriously.

'Don't talk nonsense,' Dickson said.

'From where will you supply those thousands of men when Colonel Zargham doesn't want to involve the police?'

'We will have to involve the police,' Bartosz said.

'Absolutely not!' Zargham said sternly. ' The police will not be able to save me or my family from Li Yu Ka's vengeance.'

'Then nothing can be done,' Bartosz said disappointedly.

'This is exactly what I want. That nothing should happen,' said Zargham.

It was quiet for a while and then suddenly Imran laughed loudly: 'You are all idiots! I consider you all to be donkeys!' And then he sprang into the darkness. The echo of his laugh slowly died down.

'Has he really lost it?' Dickson said. 'Or is he Li Yu Ka himself?'

No one answered. The light from their torches pierced through the darkness, but it failed to reveal any signs of Imran.

Chapter 19

THE FOLLOWING MORNING, EVERYONE, including guests and family, were eagerly waiting for Colonel Zargham. He had gone alone to Devgarhi with the packet of papers. Everyone tried to tell him that it was not safe for him to go alone but the colonel was not ready to take anyone along. There was no trace of Imran since the previous night. They had searched hard and long amongst the rocks, but they eventually gave up and returned.

Even Sophiya was surprised at this strange act of Imran's, but she did not say anything to anyone.

At about ten o'clock Zargham returned. His face showed signs of weariness. He sat down on a chair and stretched his arms.

'What happened?' Dickson asked.

'Nothing. The area was completely deserted. I placed the packet in a safe location and came back,' Zargham said. After some time he said, 'If I have returned safely, it means Li Yu Ka will not harm me or my family.'

He was about to continue when they all heard Imran's laughter. He entered the room swinging his hands and toting his air gun by his side. At that moment, his face reflected more foolishness than it normally did.

'Wah, Colonel sahib!' he laughed again. 'God forbid... No, in fact, I should say, praise the Lord! You are indeed a very intelligent man!'

'What's the matter?' the colonel looked very annoyed.

'Is this the packet you left there?' Imran said, pulling out a brown packet from his pocket.

'What! What have you done!' Zargham sprang up.

Imran tore the packet and emptied the contents on the floor, 'You should be ashamed of trying to joke with Li Yu Ka! In spite of that, he has allowed you to live!'

A mass of papers spread over the floor haphazardly. The colonel bent over the papers in a bewildered manner.

'But!' he said after a few moments. 'I left the papers there. Why did you pick them up?'

'Because I am Li Yu Ka!' Imran thundered.

'You... *You*!' the colonel stuttered. Everyone's jaw dropped. And instead of foolishness, Imran's face showed ferocity.

'Mr Bartosz, last night you were telling us schemes to capture me. I want to kill *you* first.'

'What's this insolence!' Bartosz said, turning to Zargham. 'I cannot tolerate this obnoxious secretary of yours.' Then he turned to Dickson, 'I prefer to stay in some hotel. This obnoxious secretary has been insolent towards me from the very beginning!'

'Zargham!' Dickson said. 'Tell this impudent secretary to ask forgiveness.'

'Mr Bartosz,' Imran said in a sharp tone. 'Excuse

me, but you will not be able to swallow the packet of real papers. It would be better if you hand them to me.'

'What do you mean?' Colonel Zargham started again.

Bartosz's hand went to his pocket but at the same instant, Imran's air gun fired. Bartosz jumped back, letting out a cry. A fountain of blood erupted from his arm.

Suddenly he jumped at Imran who swiftly moved aside. Bartosz ran into the wall with full force. Imran smacked his bottom with the butt of the air-gun and said, 'Confucius once said...'

Bartosz turned again. This time he was heading for the door.

'What is going on!' a cry tore out from Zargham's throat. At that very moment, Inspector Khalid entered the room and seized Bartosz by his waist as he tried to escape. Even though Bartosz's arm had been broken, he struggled so powerfully that he managed to shove Khalid off.

This time Imran smacked Bartosz's head with the butt of the gun and said, 'What else did Confucius say besides this?'

Bartosz's head spun and he tumbled over. Imran lifted him by the collar.

'Look here at the face of Li Yu Ka, who has been deceiving the world for the last two hundred years.'

'You have gone mad!' Dickson yelled.

Imran paid no heed to him and turned to Khalid. 'Retrieve that original packet of papers from him.'

During this time, hordes of uniformed personnel and armed constables had gathered inside and outside the building.

Imran put Bartosz on a chair.

Upon searching him, indeed, a brown sealed packet was recovered. Khalid took it into his custody.

Bartosz was looking faint. He closed his eyes.

'What proof do you have that he is Li Yu Ka?' Dickson said.

'Aha! Colonel,' Imran said. 'What did he say last night? Li Yu Ka will get these papers himself, right? He was right. He did get them himself. Therefore, no one else but he could be Li Yu Ka. Last night he talked in that way to gain your confidence. Why, Colonel, you prepared the packet in his presence, right?'

'All of them were present,' Zargham said, licking his dry lips.

'I suspected him the day he took me to the rocks on a hunt for herbs and upon my return I found Sophiya gone. In any case, last night he got hold of the original packet and replaced it with this one. Dickson, when did he become your friend?'

'Three years back. When he was based in London.'

'Take away Shifton, Inspector,' Imran told Khalid. 'Shifton or Li Yu Ka. You have arrested a major criminal—one who had the world dancing to his tune for two hundred years.'

'I don't understand the two hundred year thing,' Khalid said.

'For now, just take him away. Meet me in two

hours—the report will be ready,' said Imran. 'At all events, *you* have arrested Li Yu Ka. There should be no mention of Ali Imran, MSc, PhD, anywhere in the report.'

Chapter 20

AT LEAST FOR COLONEL Zargham, that evening was very pleasant. Dickson's face still showed signs of shock and disbelief even after he was convinced that it was indeed Li Yu Ka in Bartosz's guise. No one knew if his agitation was because of the events that had occurred or because of the embarrassment of bringing Zargham's enemy to his house as a guest.

On the tea table, Sophiya's laughter seemed particularly hearty. During all this time, this was perhaps the first instance when she was laughing so exuberantly. Imran's face showed the same old foolishness.

'I still can't figure out the two hundred year thing,' Zargham said, looking at Imran.

'Two hundred years are nothing. With the procedure he had adopted, his name would have lived on for thousands of years,' Imran said, shaking his head. 'Li Yu Ka was just a name which was adopted by different people, generation after generation. It was a very strange procedure. No one nominated his own child as the successor. It was Li Yu Ka's personal choice. Before passing out of this world, he nominated someone from his own group—and he chose someone only when he was absolutely sure he himself was about to die soon. Then the new Li Yu Ka followed in the predecessor's footsteps. I think I did not give Bartosz an opportunity to name a successor, so we must assume that the world has been wiped clean of Li Yu Ka's existence.'

'But we might not escape from the revenge of Li Yu Ka's gang,' Dickson said in a husky voice.

'Absolutely not!' Imran said, smiling. 'Each member of the Li Yu Ka gang is at least a millionaire. Consider the gang broken. When Li Yu Ka was alive, his terror constantly hovered over his gang members and they were worse than slaves. The reason for his terror had to do with the fact that he always stayed in the dark. I know very well that for the last twenty five years, his gang has been ready to rebel against him. So you shouldn't worry. No one from the Li Yu Ka gang will harm you.'

'But how did you figure out that Bartosz was Li Yu Ka?' the colonel asked.

'I suspected him the day he took me to the rocks in search of herbs. After that I had been pursuing him constantly, and last night, I saw him stabbing that dagger into the door frame.'

'Oh!' Zargham's eyes grew bigger.

'But Imran sahib! Why did you let Inspector Khalid take credit for your success?' Sophiya asked.

'It's a long story,' Imran said, drawing a deep breath. 'I don't want my name to be connected with this.'

'But why?'

'Haha! My mom is a very Eastern type of a woman and my dad is one hundred percent Englishman. So while he often prefers walking out of disagreements, my mom, may God increase her tribe, picks up her slippers and then I lose track of everything...how far I am from the equator...or even ordinary things such as the multiplication table for twenty.'

'Lad, you are a very dangerous man.' Colonel Zargham smiled. 'But what kind of a monster is your air gun? It broke Bartosz's arm!'

'How should I explain,' Imran said gloomily. 'I am sick of it. Sometimes, it even starts firing point two bore bullets! Isn't it absurd?'

Chapter 21

THREE DAYS LATER, THE papers published a report credited to Inspector Khalid, in which all the events starting from the acquisition of some mysterious papers by Colonel Zargham to the present arrests were narrated. In the end it said that if Colonel Zargham wasn't ignorant of Chinese and Japanese and if the papers had landed with someone who knew both these languages, then much would have already been discovered about Li Yu Ka's personality. Among these papers was also a report of a Chinese investigator, which was written for the Chinese Investigation Bureau's Headquarters. It was mentioned in this report that Li Yu Ka was not Japanese but a Czechoslovakian. According to Inspector Khalid's statement, the identity of the Chinese man who handed the papers to Colonel Zargham remained a mystery. Nothing could be said with any surety about him: whether he was the investigator who wrote this report or if he was someone from Li Yu Ka's gang who had tried to get these papers from the investigator and send them to Li Yu Ka.

There was no reference to Imran in Inspector Khalid's report. But Imran himself had prepared it.

After regaining consciousness, not only did Bartosz accept the allegations, he also clarified that after him there wouldn't be another Li Yu Ka. The wound on his head proved fatal and he died before he could give any further information about himself.

Acknowledgements

I'D LIKE TO THANK Musharraf Ali Farooqi, Urdu's premier translator into English, for his unbridled support for this project in particular and my work in general. He has always been a ready friend and mentor.

Special thanks to Ahmad Safi, who meticulously studied the drafts for errors. He was generous with my foibles, misreadings and clunky word choices, and suggested better alternatives.

Thanks to Chiki Sarkar, my editor, who made this translation work in English and for her support for this project.

I'd also like to thank Dr. Frances Pritchett for allowing me to use her translations of Ghalib's verses from her website www.columbia.edu/~fp7 , one of the best resources for Urdu-wallahs on the web.

My deepest gratitude, of course, is for my mother, for her prayers.

A Note on the Author

Ibn-e Safi was born in 1928 in India. He created two great mystery series, *Jasoosi Duniya* and the Imran series during the 1950s. Both gained massive popularity and were translated into several languages. Ibn-e safi died of pancreatic cancer on his birthday on July 26, 1980 in Karachi.

A Note on the Translator

Bilal Tanweer is an author and translator. This is his first book-length work of translation. He is working on his first novel and another book of translation.